DICEY

Also by Faye Green:

The Boy on the Wall

DICEY

June,
Thank you for your
support and your
friendship.
Love
Faye

FAYE GREEN

authorHOUSE®

AuthorHouse™
1663 Liberty Drive
Bloomington, IN 47403
www.authorhouse.com
Phone: 1-800-839-8640

Dicey is a work of fiction. Names, characters, places and incidents are the product of the author's imagination or are used fictitiously. Any resemblance to actual events, locales or persons, living or dead, is coincidental.

Published by AuthorHouse   03/14/2013

ISBN: 978-1-4817-2800-3 (sc)
ISBN: 978-1-4817-2801-0 (e)

Library of Congress Control Number: 2013904594

Any people depicted in stock imagery provided by Thinkstock are models, and such images are being used for illustrative purposes only.
Certain stock imagery © Thinkstock.

This book is printed on acid-free paper.

For my children, Billy and Julie

ACKNOWLEDGEMENTS

Writing a novel was a solitary task. The story poured forth but if it were not for the supportive people around me, it would most likely still be resting on my computer. First is my husband, Bill, who admonished me to *just do it,* in his matter of fact way of always expecting me to move on with every goal I set for myself. His constant love sustained me and I am sure that he would be proud that I have continued after his death.

My dear friend, Penny Reuss, asked to read my work and from that day, insisted on reading every page I write. She became my cheerleader. Her faith in this books, and the others I have written, is unshakable. Every author needs someone like Penny, an avid reader who can compare your work to classic and contemporary authors and honestly critique it. It is fair to say this book would not be in hand if not for her.

I want to acknowledge and thank those who read *Dicey* for me. They encouraged me and helped me to believe in this book. Michelle Kruhm, Vickie Bennett, Joy Knox, Claudette Latsko, Rita Ryor, Marylou McCue, Sue Faulkner and Peggy Andrews. Thank you for reading and doing invaluable proofing, too

I am grateful for my editor, Connie Rinehold. Her expertise has polished *Dicey.* I have learned so much from her and our association has been delightful. Connie was easy to work with, generous with her time and a consummate professional.

I would like to acknowledge the ladies and gentlemen in my writers' group, the Delmarva Christian Writers Fellowship. They have become mentors to me, led by Candy Abbott, who in her quiet manner, divides and shares herself in such an unselfish manner. You know who you are and I appreciate your support at each monthly meeting.

Lynn Taylor, you proved the truth in this work of fiction and that is what this author hoped to portray.

Finally, Richard.

CHAPTER 1

It is hard to say which shocked her more, getting the call from David to come to his hospital room or the wad of money he pressed into her hand as soon as she got to his bedside. The slight smile that crossed his handsome face told her to be quiet about the transaction. She looked across the room where a group of strangers were quietly talking.

He whispered the nick name he had given her years ago, "Dicey."

Are these his family? She wondered as he emphatically pointed his index finger at her and then, with his thumb, indicated the door. His only words: "The apartment" There was no doubt; he wanted her to leave immediately. She did.

Delores Grant was the same age as the man in the hospital bed but her life had been easier and she looked younger. Her curly brown hair did not need the attention of a hair stylist to color it. It was naturally highlighted and softly outlined a pretty face that was easily given to smiles and gentle wrinkles around her green eyes. She dressed neatly and attracted attention as if she was the most important person entering your space. From across the room she was often mistaken for a much younger woman, but when approached, her laughing eyes removed age from her equation.

Five minutes ago she, with great trepidation, had entered the Greater Laurel Beltsville Hospital. All that worry, and now she was heading out the fancy self-opening door with a knot of money in her raincoat, and without facing the things that had concerned her as she drove one hundred miles to get here. "It's about geography; when I am in Maryland, I am a different person," she said aloud as was her habit. Coming home to familiar roads, passing the former schools and homes made her revisit old feelings, especially after seeing David. Memories came forward and David presented old topography. In Delaware she could deny her feelings; seeing him again, especially so compromised, made her heart ache. Questions were swimming in her head and she hardly remembered finding and entering her car. *Why is David in the hospital? Why all those tubes and machines?* The weird occurrences at his bedside delayed her worry about this special man. Now, she faced her fears about his fate and wondered if he was dying. She dared not take the bulge from her pocket for fear that someone may see it. She patted her side to feel the bundle and started the car.

"Oh, David. What do you want of me now? As much as you hate explaining yourself, this time you will." She said to the rear view mirror. Dicey drove to I-95 and headed south to David's apartment. The key was on her key ring and she wondered if it would open the door that she had not approached for almost six years. The key slid into the latch and turned with such ease Dicey felt a twinge of pleasure. She entered with the same ease with which she and David had brought their lives together intermittently through the years.

The quiet, empty rooms shook her to the core. The apartment had her touch; she had helped him to furnish it when he came from the hospital after his open-heart surgery fifteen years ago. He had called her to come then, too

Oh, David. Don't you dare die. What if he did? What would she do with this huge unfinished part of her life? Even as the years passed, she never thought death would remove any chance for a life together.

The phone rang as she closed the door. As she had been taught, she let it go to the answering machine, her hand poised to pick it up if it was David. It was not.

"Dave, do you want to see me or not . . . it is up to you. Call." That call was hardly finished, when another ringing startled her. A second gruff male voice made demands. "What's the story? What the hell am I to do? Call me on my cell. Obviously you aren't answering yours." Dicey fell into the chair trying to think. She knew they were David's customers but she was not sure what she was to do about them. She stood up and walked into the kitchen; the only thing she could decide was to make coffee. The aroma wafted through the apartment and gave her some comfort as she gathered a cup and went to the refrigerator to get some creamer. A note in David's smooth, fluid handwriting stopped her at the counter.

Her legs buckled and she slowly folded to the floor as she read quickly, then again, more slowly, tears tracking down her face and off her chin:

Dice, No one knows about the apartment. I will get three calls. They are collections. Make an appointment with each to meet. You've seen me make collections before. It's set up. Just tell them you are Dicey and it will go fine. What would I do without you?

Love, D.

Well, you manage to do very well without me. Years on end. She remembered his hand gesture in the hospital, abrupt and sharp, like an order—the forefinger pointed at her. She knew that gesture—*go*, it pointed . . . *to the apartment.* And then, the smile—*love.* For the second time today, her ears heard her lament, "Oh, David." Dicey stayed on the floor drinking black coffee, forgetting the creamer.

She pulled herself together finally rising to refill her cup adding cream and sugar to let the richness and sweetness infuse her. She gathered her thoughts and dismissed the panic feelings. "David is strong," she assured herself as she picked her coat up from the floor, once again touching the pocket. The money caused the usual *pukey* feeling in her gut. David's money always did that to her. Normally when Dicey came back to her hometown, she called a friend or checked into the Hampton Inn right off Route 198. Her family and David's had lived in Laurel, Maryland for generations. They were neighborhood kids. The small town had mushroomed about the time they graduated from high school, as did the beefing up at the nearby military post, Ft George G. Meade.

Dicey and David started their adult lives on the same page, each finding spouses, marrying and living in the typical brick ranchers near the homes of their parents. David suddenly went in a different direction. When he divorced his high school sweetheart, David's and Dicey's lives were poles apart. Dicey continued the conventional path; he chose to step to the other side of his love of gambling, and became a bookie. His sudden switch to a flashy lifestyle was not lost on the gossipy hometown where the core of 'ole Laurel' families still followed its sons and daughters. The unexplained became a topic for coffee klatches and barstool banter.

Dicey sat holding her coffee, with the coat draped across her knees, while she called her daughter.

"Hi Jen, I came to Laurel today. How are my beautiful granddaughters?"

"Mom! They are fine; we all are. Are you coming up to Frederick?"

"Maybe this weekend. I'm here because one of my classmates is ill and I came to see him."

"Who? Wait . . . let me guess . . ."

"David," she interrupted. "I only saw him for a moment. He's in the hospital."

"Oh, Mom. Are you going to be involved again like when he had the heart problem? How about his other friends? Let his son take care of him."

"Actually, Jen, I don't really know what his problem is. His son may be here; I wouldn't know him if I saw him. I'll stay over tonight and see if I can find out tomorrow. Don't worry about me. I don't have anything else going on. I'm not getting involved!" Censoring the meager information she gave Jen was hard. A quick draft of caffeine gave her a boost. "I'm staying at his apartment while he is in the hospital. If you need me, call my cell." Dicey hated lying to Jen about getting involved. Taking care of David's money and phone calls was definitely *involvement*. She promised herself to explain when she knew why she was lying.

"Mom, I hope we don't have all that mystery again. No undisclosed trips. I know you love the excitement when you are around David but you are older now, I hate to remind you." She finished with a bit of humor in her voice.

"Thanks, dear, but you know I never use age as an excuse for anything, and I hope you won't either. Look at all I could have missed, especially since your father died."

Jen changed the subject as this was going in an old direction, down an old road they had traveled before. "We want to see you before you go home."

"Not much use in driving there when everyone is at work or school. Good night, Jen. I'll decide tomorrow and call you."

Jen's sigh of frustration came through loud and clear. "Mom, where is the apartment? Tell me that, at least." She asked quickly.

"Don't worry. Everything will be fine, I'm sure. I'm as close as the phone and I will call you every day." She ignored Jen's inquiry.

"Let me know how it goes for David." Jen cared about him but her real concern was for her mother. "I love, you, Mom."

Dicey knew Jen was upset. She could not give her daughter assurances that she did not have, but she tried to project a confidence which she did not have either. She hung up the phone, feeling terrible.

Now Dicey faced the problem in her coat pocket and remembered the safe that was snuggled behind the hot water heater, looking like ductwork. The combination, the date they graduated from Laurel High School, worked like a charm. The money was stashed, she did not have to touch it again, and that felt good. The television provided background, and a grilled cheese took the edge off her hunger. She avoided looking at the phone that was blinking a bright red three, reminding her of the phone calls she must deal with tomorrow. She put that off just as she avoided going into her bedroom until sleep became her overwhelming desire. The room was well prepared. All the familiar furnishings were polished and the bed was dressed with fresh linens as if she had recently been here. David was neat in his habits and she was not surprised. A small box of Godiva chocolates was on the bedside table with a one-word note in his handwriting—*Dicey*. There was no doubt, the room was carefully prepared for the woman standing holding the candy.

She dressed for bed without opening the closet; she did not want to look at the contents, which would unnerve her. She stared at it the double doors and turned away. She did not want to see the flashy dresses worn in Las Vegas or the fur coat they fought about because she would not take it home to Delaware. The red shoes would be lined up as reminders of the past. Too many memories, too many secrets, she decided. Morning would be soon enough to deal all that and . . . more worry.

The thoughts running through her restless sleep were a disturbing confusion of happy times and concern about her lifetime friend, lying in the hospital. The last dream was a nightmare of David dead and a storm with lightning and money pouring from the sky.

The cell phone on the bedside table wiggled and jumped, insisting she wake. The clock said 7:05 as she angled up on one elbow and answered.

David said, "Dicey, I need to talk to you."

5

"You sure do. Why are you in the hospital? What is . . ."

"Dice, I only have a minute. Why didn't you come back to the hospital after visiting hours last night? Are you all right? I have been worried sick."

"You worried about me? I am not the one in the hospital. I didn't know I was supposed to come back."

"I should have known you wouldn't open the bundle I gave you. Damn. There is a note to you. OK . . . OK . . . I have to quickly tell you a couple of things. I'm having surgery soon and after that I will be in an induced coma for about three days. Can you stay in Maryland?"

"Surgery? Coma? What's wrong?" She drew one long breath. "Of course, I can stay."

"Here is the wrinkle. Stay away from my hospital room. Don't introduce yourself to anyone. I don't know who will come during visiting hours while I am . . . out . . . but you must not come and run into anyone."

"David, what are you talking about? What kind of surgery?"

"Read the note. Take care of things. Come to the hospital this morning but not to the surgery waiting room. Suzette will be here. Patrick, too. Got it?" She knew Patrick was his son and she could guess who Suzette was.

"Mr. King, give me the phone, I'm starting the IV drip now . . ." The phone went dead.

Rolling over in the bed should be comforting to Dicey, but it was not. She never felt so alone nor so longed for her quiet existence back in Delaware. Her life there was a lot like the lay of the land—flat, even, and smooth—a surface without bends and curves. Living in a retirement community that included a clubhouse and many friends who are ready to do happy hour, dine out, attend movies, and go on short excursions was where she should be, right now, on a quiet, even plane with a comfortable life.

Not today, she reminded herself. If she'd really wanted all that peace and sameness, she would have stayed in Delaware.

The desire to run home passed as she jumped out of bed and fed the safe the numbers that opened the door. His treasure was in her hands, which were shaking as she took the band off and watched all large bills cover her feet. The note was right where he said it would be.

Dice, put the money in the safe. Come back to the hospital after visiting hours. I will explain. You will be comfortable in my apartment. Stay there, everything is set up for you. Use the money if you need anything and please make arrangements to stay in Maryland for the week. Write this number down—301 555-1276—Dr. Drysdale. Talk to him; he will explain. Keep it handy.

I love you. David.

There it was—the elephant in Dicey's life. She was dependable, upbeat, and loyal—just the person to be called in times of trouble. She loved him but was it enough for all this? Could she handle his illness; his business and all this mystery?

David's life was exciting, way too serious, and always changing. At times, he called her for a dose of her humor and honesty.

Usually she could sense when things were not going well and she could give him *something* over the phone. She thought of the calls she got from him while he was in prison. He knew that she would not be forever prejudiced against him. She noticed his conversations were changing and beginning to express a philosophy on life that was way beyond his lifestyle and occupation. He was reading everything he could about the human condition: the Bible, Voltaire, Darwin, Freud, C.F. Lewis, even Homer. In 14 months, he had changed. She went to see him when he got out of prison and found he was the same in every way, except this. He had reconciled his life; every day he risked everything, except his innermost being and his self-respect. He understood freedom because he had lived without it. He understood—there was no justice, only concessions and politics. David separated man and God and expected very little from the former and everything from the latter. He decided not to lie about anything. David and Dicey were different in every way except this. They shared a philosophy and it came to each from different parts of the universe. He understood this; she only felt it. This new man had redeemed himself in her eyes and she was once again, after a span of many middle years, willing to renew her feelings for him. Dicey was the settled, reliable, responsible type and no one knew that better than David. He was complex and she understood him. The real irony was the part of her that would hold on to this man and his foreign world even while she was happy and fulfilled in her own. Dicey often wondered if everyone had a side that wanted the adventure usually produced in Hollywood. She would never forfeit her life but, felt most fortunate to be a close observer of David's. For the last seventeen years, he had relied on her, called on her and depended on her, and he expected her to be there for him. She made a life in retirement without a husband and without David until his heart problems. She was his best friend, mostly on the phone, except three trips when he needed a woman to travel with him. She asked nothing of him and refused to accept money or gifts.

Their mutual lifetime friends knew they had a special alliance but had no idea of the relationship that seemed to *just happen* after she was widowed. Dicey was still deep in her grief and loneliness when David called before he had open-heart surgery and she went to him because of her debilitating loneliness. His need was a balm to her injured spirit and the easy friendship was medicine to her soul. They bonded in every way except sexually; her grief was too fresh.

He asked her to come to his bed once; she declined and he did not ask again. As time went by, her feelings toward him became more intense and harder to define, but he never called her for what she wanted most to do for him. Dicey knew he was protecting her; that his life could put her in jeopardy.

In her younger days she might have been impetuous and tied her life tightly to his but she was not that young and reckless now. David was a dangerous man. She knew it was important to keep all of his secrets, especially their hidden relationship. She welcomed their interludes, but, this was not the time for such excitement and mystery.

Jen is right, I am too old for this and should not get involved, she laughed as she thought it. She was already up to her neck in David's problems and up to her ankles in his money.

*   *   *

David and Delores were in the second grade together and he was the most annoying critter on the earth, sitting behind her using her pigtails as his distraction to the lessons. Surely, school meant more than putting up with this boy. His mother was the room mother and so sweet at class parties. How could she have such a bad boy? The days he was absent were her happiest and when, in mid-February, he was absent for two weeks, she thought maybe he had died and she was rid of him. What did a seven-year-old girl know about death and wishing for it? He did not die, but his mother did. Mrs. Brown prepared the class for his return. In her sing-songy voice she announced, "David's mother died. He is returning to class tomorrow. We must all be very kind to him." Was that preparation? The tailspin of feelings that washed over the little pigtailed girl never left, even after many years. She must be a very bad girl, wishing for his death and his mother died. Delores began to cry inconsolably and suffered great embarrassment, which seemed to bring more flooding tears. "Could my mother die, before I get home today?" she wondered. Mrs. Brown sent her to the principal's office, but she did not know what to do with the crying child either. Delores ran home that day and hugged her mother long and hard, but did not tell her why. The next day David and Delores were seated in line four, seats five and six, as if his mother was not dead and she had not cried in school yesterday. He was not interested in her pigtails and she did not, for one moment, forget that he was back there, leaving her hair alone. Delores wanted him to pull her braids or put paper bits and erasers into them. It was the beginning of wanting something from him that would last for decades. Someone told him that she had cried for his mother, and so they became friends. He resumed pulling her hair and now she missed him and his attention when he was absent. For the rest of their primary school years, Delores told him arithmetic answers and shared her lunch if he forgot his. David told her about his mother. They did not play together; he played with the boys, but she had a place in his life. Somehow, she helped him with the loss of his mother.

"What is the answer to number seven."

"Forty-six"

"Delores, where do you think my mother is right now?" He asked as if she had that answer as easily as the division problems they were doing.

"I don't know, David. I don't even know where my mother is right now."

"But she will be home when you get there, won't she?"

"Every day, I hope so."

"I hope my mother will be home, too." He had her to tend his broken heart, to give him answers and to assure him when neither of them had answers.

CHAPTER 2

As Dicey drove to the hospital, she wondered why he wanted her to come here this morning if he did not want her in the surgical waiting room. She had no plan as she entered the bright lobby draped in green plants and generic pictures. *Information* seemed a good place to start. "Could you tell me what room David King will be in when his surgery is over this morning?"

"One moment. Let's see. He will be in intensive care for at least 4 days. There is no room assignment. Only family will be admitted there, one at a time." She turned to leave when the receptionist said, "There is a note on this patient file. Are you Delores Grant?"

"Yes."

"I am to page Dr. Drysdale. Will you have a seat?"

"Isn't Dr. Drysdale in surgery with Mr. King?"

"No ma'am. He is not a surgeon. Dr. Drysdale is an oncologist."

I do not want to talk to an oncologist; I want to run, her mind screamed as she groped behind her for a chair. Dicey was a person of action and waiting for answers left her limp. Oncologists never give more than a pittance of hope.

She took a seat and wondered how many more questions would be presented before any answers came. The brightness in the hospital lobby belied the dark cloud that was coming over the pleasantly decorated lobby with the mention of oncology. That word had a force that tore her fiber and prompted a flashback. In a Nano-second the scans, chemo bags, suffering and the last day that marked the end of her husband's existence become part of this day.

The man in a white coat, holding a clip board, walked across the lobby and approached her. "Ms. Grant, I am John Drysdale. Will you come with me?" He led her to a small comfortable well-appointed room intended for doctor/patient/family conferences. "You are Mr. King's . . . friend ?" The doctor could not hide his curiosity, recalling that his patient had not been clear on their relationship. Her engaging smile put him at ease.

"Dr. Drysdale. I am his longtime friend. Not a significant other or anything like that."

"He has left you a lot of responsibility; you must be a very good friend," he said pensively. "I have Mr. King's living will. I am clear on his desires." He handed her a sheaf of papers. "In our discussions he said you would be here. My notes say you and Patrick King are to be notified if we have to institute his final wishes." He was quiet while she read the living will.

It was a relief to be reading a document, using the mind and keeping it from running wild. David wanted nothing done to keep him alive. No food. No water. No respirator. Do not resuscitate. Not all unlike her own.

"Will I have to do anything?"

"No. He is in surgery starting about now," he said glancing at his watch. "Will you stay at the hospital until it is over? I believe his son is in the surgical waiting room. It is a dangerous procedure but we are very confident; he will come through fine." Dicey took those words and held on to them.

Oh God. Oh David! She thought. Looking up at the doctor, she found her voice. "I have not seen him in a while and I have no idea what his medical condition is. I don't even know why he is in surgery."

The doctor's voice softened. "His surgery today is for a brain tumor we believe to be benign. We are trying to remove it without loss of any faculties. It is in an area which controls sight. Without this surgery, he would be blind very soon." He reached out and took her hand. "Mr. King will be fine. His pre-ops were good; his doctor is the best. Let's keep a positive attitude."

"I'm trying, Doctor."

He gave her a moment and saw her resolve strength straighten her back and bring a slight smile for him.

"There is something else . . ."

Dicey sighed and allowed her shoulders to drop into a yielding stance. What else could this man tell her? Surely he gave her the worst news first and what he was about to say would not be more terrible than brain surgery or possibly executing David's living will. "Mr. King said you would be able to pay for his care; he came without insurance. Do not misunderstand . . . . he didn't say you were responsible for his bill, just that you had access to his resources and would pay with his funds. Is that correct?"

"Dr. Drysdale, I trust you will hold this in strict confidence. The means to pay for Mr. King's care is available but I desire that my part in it be kept from his family and his other doctors. I am in a very tenuous position and I fear that communication between Mr. King and his son is not good. I do not know him and he knows nothing of me and could challenge my control over Mr. King's monies and his trust in me. The name Delores Grant means nothing to his son or others waiting for word from this surgery, and it must stay that way. I am here to help keep his affairs in order until he can resume management of them. Hopefully, he will regain consciousness and be able to handle everything. If that does not happen, I assure you, his bills will be paid."

"Thank you, Ms. Grant. Now may I escort you to the surgical waiting area?"

"No. It is best that I not be where the family is waiting. Can I remain here? Will you keep me informed?" As the doctor took the door, she rose to touch his arm.

"Is there anything else?" She asked, afraid of his answer.

"Did I mention he will be kept in a coma for several days and will not be able to see you?"

"That is the one thing I did know, Doctor. You will be my only contact until David can talk to me. My cell number is on this card. Call me anytime."

Dr. Drysdale left after the most unusual conversation that he had had in his years in this profession. He was impressed. If he had to trust a stranger, this composed lady was an excellent choice. Mr. King had done well in selecting someone to act in his stead. There must be a good story behind their relationship.

In the quiet of the private waiting room, sleep finally caught up with Dicey and she woke with a start as the information clerk entered calling her name. "Ms. Grant, Doctor Drysdale is on the phone for you. Pick up that receiver and press three."

"Hello, Doctor. Delores Grant. How is Mr. King," she asked, afraid for the answer.

"So far; so good. He came through the operation fine. His heart did a good job for him; all vitals are stable. We are moving him to intensive care as we speak."

"Is he still going to be in the coma for the next few days?"

"Yes, that was predetermined and the necessity is unchanged. I have your number and if I need you; I will call. Are you alright; do you need anything?"

"Can I call you tomorrow to see how David is doing?"

The gentle assurances and kindness of the doctor was the only comfort Dicey found in this day. The afternoon sun cast long shadows as she left the cocoon of her little room with the crumbs of information gleaned at the hospital. The thought of returning to the apartment alone dimmed her spirit even more. Food was her next thought. She had almost reached the door when someone took her arm and spun her around while speaking her name.

"Delores. Did you come to see David?" he asked.

She was looking into the eyes of another member of their graduating class. Allen Herbert was walking beside her and talking fast. Al and David played varsity football together eons ago. "I waited through surgery but I couldn't see him. Did you?" Quick thinking was usually her forte but the highly charged emotions of the last 24 hours left her without a fabrication to answer Al's question.

He was such a loud, quick talker that he did not wait for her answer and drew his own conclusions. They passed out the door as if they had a place to go together. "I didn't see you in the waiting room. Just me, David's son and Suzette." He made the assumption that she knew Suzette. "We are all so relieved that he came through. Suzette said his heart had a good checkup."

That was a bit of good news, but who was this *Suzette*?

"Patrick said he has a long incision . . . ." He drew his finger across his head above the left ear. "A brain tumor is a scary thing."

Her knees were weak and her heart was racing. She needed the arm that was holding her and helping her to walk.

"Come over to the Green Turtle with me. Hungry?"

"I am starved." Dicey finally found her voice, to speak to this old friend. She needed any information he might have and his company was better than a long lonely evening with a cheese sandwich. "How have you been, Al? How is Anna? I haven't seen you two since our last reunion six years ago." She tried small talk before turning the conversation to what he knew about David's health. They headed into the dimly lit pub and ordered two beers and sandwiches.

Dicey was still doing concentrated breathing as she slowly tasted hers and decided what to say. "Al, I really didn't know about David's surgery; I was visiting my aunt today. Tell me what you know."

Al loved the invitation to talk and began describing what he knew about David. Dicey paid close attention as he told of the suspected benign tumor in a sensitive area of the brain. The swelling after surgery would make him very uncomfortable, possibly deaf and blind until the swelling subsided. That was why he was in a coma and the doctors are going to keep him there. "They say he will be fine, and I hope they are right."

She wanted to ask why there was an oncologist on David's case but did not. It could be that David had not told others about Dr. Drysdale. She was always careful about giving information about David and she did not want to say anything that would lead Al to know that she was privy to something he did not know. Al ordered another beer; Dicey passed. The beers loosened Al's tongue. She let him ramble on, trying to glean any information she could. He talked of the woman, Suzette, and revealed that she was David's latest girlfriend, just as Dicey supposed. David lived with her for about three years. Dicey was sure the woman had never been to the apartment and surmised this girlfriend was not trusted.

The sandwiches came just as Al was about to tell her about David's call to him yesterday. Trying to act nonchalant, she let the food delay his story, deciding to take him back to it as soon as possible. Their meal was suddenly interrupted by Al's quick bolt from his chair to meet a woman coming into the restaurant. He led her back to their table saying,

"Suzette, this is a friend of mine and David's, too. Delores Grant. We went to high school together."

"How do you do," she said in a distinct French accent. It was like a comedy ballet as the ever-bumbling Al introduced David's women to each other, using dumb words and stupid definitions to define the dancers. "Delores is one of our oldest friends. Suzette, is David's wo . . . . girlfriend."

The woman, at least twenty years their junior, had deeply tanned skin and the lovely features of many island women. Dicey was struck by her beauty as she studied the woman's face to see if her name sparked any special curiosity. It did not. Obviously, David had never mentioned Dicey to Suzette. It was one of those moments when she wished to be transported mystically from this place to some distant plane. *I should not be here.* Dicey thought but said nothing, letting Al fill in all the awkward moments with his chatter. While drink and food was ordered for the new guest, Dicey concentrated on finishing her sandwich so she could make the exit she wanted so badly. She had great fear that she might say something that would betray David's desire to have her presence invisible. As much as she wanted to know what David told Al yesterday; she had to go, almost as if she could see David s's finger and thumb signals given to her yesterday at his bedside. Al was sometimes foolish, and she would not want him to make reference to their special friendship.

Dicey finally made her goodbyes after answering Al's final question. "Will you still be in Maryland when David wakes?"

"I am driving to Frederick to spend time with Jen and the family. Not sure what my plans are after that." One of the best things about Al was that he didn't care about your answers to his questions. She left without getting all the information she wanted, but she was sure it was too risky to stay with these two.

*   *   *

The close years of Elementary School vanished for David and Delores as they moved on to the junior high years. She chose to excel in her studies and become a class leader; David used his brain to scoff at the subjects and cram for the exams. He had a good brain or he would never have passed from grade to grade with so little effort. Delores's friends did not expect her to spend time with him and his friends felt the same about her. But, they did spend time together whenever he was in trouble or danger of failing for not turning in his assignments. She simply could not resist the appeal he made for her time and homework. All of the girls wanted David's attention; she was no different. The first time she came upon him shooting craps at the side of the schoolyard, he looked up with those warm, smiling brown eyes and asked her to roll the dice for him. He held the dice out to her and said, "For luck," David laughed; he knew she would not do it. For her refusal and scorn of his game he gave her the name 'Dicey', which to him meant stuck up. It also referred to something that he would hook his future to—dice. The irony was that he also hooked his future to Dicey, and she was more reliable than the dice and not at all the real definition of the word dicey which meant iffy or on thin ice.

CHAPTER 3

Being comatose presented a mystery to David. He could not fathom yielding control over his life but, he had no choice. The probability that he would hear those around him, and not remember anything, was real. His first thought, when the necessity for the induced coma was explained, was *get Dicey here.* She would come. No doubt about it. Dicey was a part of his life whenever his own bestial force could not get him over troubled waters. She would make the impossible possible.

As he came into the shallows of the anesthesia, he remembered telling Dicey to stay away from this sterile world. *I want her here,* his silence screamed. David wanted to hear his mother's voice and Dicey's voice. They were confused in his mind. She would protect him, take care of him. He knew it but did not know it. None of his brute force could correct what was wrong here in this room where hard tubes filled his mouth, throat and chest.

David sank back into the black. His dream was clear; her voice was strong, pure, and unmistakable. It was Dicey. He floated into a comfort zone that allowed his muscles and defenses to relax.

"David, I am here. You will be alright; I promise." Just as he wished she would take his hand, she did. He willed his hand to grip hers but nothing moved. The dream continued. "I will be here waiting for you."

He seemed to be nothing but ears; no sight, no feeling—nothing. His aural senses were bringing her to him; it was all he had—there was nothing else.

"Remember the days in Nassau? Think about the white sand, the sea and the cool drinks we had." He tried to remember. Yes. Yes. The beach . . . but the beach he recalled was not on an island, it was on the Chesapeake Bay. The sand was not white. A sand pail was held tight in his little hand as his father lifted him to his shoulders while his mother ran beside them. He looked at his mother but her face was turned away. He listened for her laughter but could not hear it. Panic came and then his mother spoke,

"I love you, David."

*   *   *

Dicey entered the hospital through the emergency room and followed the corridors to the elevator to the fourth floor and the intensive care unit. It was the same path she had used when her mother was dying. If the nurse in charge was compassionate, she would get in to see David. It was worth a try. The buzzer brought the duty nurse to the entry.

"Please, may I see David King for a moment?"

"It is late, are you family?"

"Not exactly."

"Family is a strange requirement these days when the most important visitors are not married to the patient. I assume you are *significant* to Mr. King? You know, he won't know you are here."

"Yes, I know."

"I am Delores Grant. Dr. Drysdale said he put me on Mr. King's visitor's list."

"Come this way. Ten minutes."

David looked helpless, peaceful, and young. Dicey took a minute to breathe and accept the scene. She cried seeing him so compromised, so without the strength he had always possessed. A silent tear trailed down her cheek.

"David, I am here. You will be alright." Her words came back to her own ears as if spoken in a vacuum and failed to give her the assurance she was trying to deliver to David. His even breathing gave her promise that he would recover, just as his hair would re-grow on the left side of his head. Dicey studied the grey at his temple and, like admitting to the reflection in a mirror, she accepted that they were both aging. A strong longing came over her as she prayed for his recovery and the chance that they might have more time. She thought of the trip they made to Nassau and began to talk to him of the warm sunny days they had spent together on the wide beaches. She finished with the words they spoke so often. "I love you."

*   *   *

High school was a passage for him. Delores loved every minute, the studies, the clubs, and the social life.

He was outstanding, not for his scholarship or sports prowess but, for his looks. David was knock-down, drag-out handsome and so well liked. His black hair and deep voice reminded the girls of Elvis. He was a man's man and women liked that. His girls were the pretty ones. When Delores and David got to high school his interest was shapely, worldly girls, and she was not one of those. They were still friends—more than friends. He was not like a brother and not a boyfriend either. Although he kissed her a time or two, they never had a date and she did not know anything about kissing back. Delores was definitely a late bloomer; David was on a fast track. Although David sought her out to talk, it never crossed his mind to take her on a date. He dared her to accept his behavior, which was foreign to a girl who would not taste beer or a cigarette. He, on the other hand, enjoyed those and so many more pleasures that would not come to her for many years. She allowed his teasing about her innocence just as she had allowed his torment via the pigtail in second grade.

Delores remembered the first time he showed her a roll of money he had won in a poker game; she refused his offer to pay for the car insurance she was saving for. They talked of everything as he tried to deal with a married woman he was in love with and the decision to marry a school sweetheart. Delores remembered the hot summer night he came to her with trouble on his mind. Something was wrong but he chose not to tell her what it was; he just wanted to be with her for a while. When he left, he thanked her but she did not know what she had done for him. Delores followed him to the car and leaned in the window as he took his wallet and pulled out a picture of his mother's pretty face. Then he kissed her hard, started the car and smiled that wonderful smile. "I'm going in the Army tomorrow. I'm scared."

"David, how are you going to make it in the Army? You hate rules"

"I can do this. I've got to. Life is full of rules; guess I had better learn to live by them. What are you going to do? Write that book? You love the rules; who is going to break them for you if I am gone?" He pulled a stray curl and said, "Sorry, I won't be here when you grow up."

Dicey was angry with him for that remark. Two weeks ago she was valedictorian but not smart enough to know she had a lot to learn.

21

CHAPTER 4

It had been a while since she had traveled with David's when he conducted business, but Dicey knew what to do. It was time to get the names from the answering machine and take care of the jobs entrusted to her by the gambler in the hospital bed. With pencil and notebook in hand, she brought up the caller ID and wrote the names and numbers. She would make these calls before opening the closet to prepare for the meetings. She needed a time and place. Arrangements had to be made without mentioning the reason for the meetings.

"This is Dicey, calling for Dave. When and where shall we meet?"

"Hi Dicey. It's Tike. Can we meet tomorrow at 12:15 at Armatucci's Italian Grill. Do you know where that is?"

"Yes. I assume noontime; I don't do midnight."

"Of course. It has been a while but I think I will recognize you. Red shoes?"

"Yes." She made the notes she would need to meet Tike and dialed the second number.

"This is Dicey, calling for Dave."

"It's about time; I'd about given up on this call." This person had an attitude and was definitely disappointed to hear from Dave or someone acting on his behalf. Dicey knew instantly that it was one of those losers who hated to pay up.

"Not a chance. Where and when? Who is this?" Each client had a code-like name.

"Tommy G. Tomorrow at noon?"

"Noon won't work for me. Earlier or later."

"2:30 at the Cinema at Columbia Circle. I'll be waiting by the fountain in front."

"Have we met? Will you know me?"

"If you wear those red shoes, I will." Click.

By the time she dialed the last number, the adrenalin was flowing. She remembered the first time she went with David to make collections in Las Vegas. David dressed in black and she in red—the same on every subsequent collection. He did not allow her ignorance; she had to know what they were doing. Collections were cash payoffs for a bet that David took and his client lost. There were rules: money had to be in an envelope, it was never counted, and no conversation. David had established his own rules about contact. This was a different situation, with his health issues and the impending coma, David had made all but three collections on last weekend's action. He instructed three clients to pay Dicey by arranging meetings on the apartment phone. Two of the losers had met her before. Dicey was sure there were rules for times when David had to pay to a winner but she had never been with him for those. She did remember that collections had to be timely. Habitual gamblers were likely to bet money they owed David on the next big thing and that could make collecting more difficult. Usually, the loser was anxious to pay off their bookie. They were too weak to hold money in their pocket, and they wanted to be able to come to David for the next sure thing.

"This is Dicey, calling for Dave."

"Ah, Yes Dicey. He told me to expect to hear from you." The voice was warm and gentlemanly, different from the other two.

"I am calling to arrange a meeting."

"Come to my office. Horton, Horton & Marquette, Suite 202, the professional building on the corner of New Hampshire and Rock Creek. You know the area? Say 5:30 tomorrow. Ask for me, Marquette."

"Yes. I'll be there." Dicey realized, too late, that she had just made a mistake. Bookies always meet on neutral ground, whether making bets or collections. David would not approve of her going to the lawyer's office.

Now she was definitely entangled. She rationalized that David would need these monies to pay the enormous hospital bill that was growing minute by minute. She was ignoring the distasteful nature of David's business, only thinking of his needs. Her soft, gentle even life in Delaware was slipping away.

The closet was just as she left it except most of the hanging items were in laundry bags with tags. She was not surprised that he freshened the clothes in the closet just as he had freshened the bed linens. A quick sweep with her hand and she saw all the familiar dresses, jackets and coats. On closer look, she saw several new pieces, in her size, in classic designs, with tags. Lined in the shoe rack were the matching shoes, including three pairs of red ones. The sight of it was heart wrenching just as she knew it would be.

She remembered how sick David was when she hung the first red dress and put the first pair of red shoes in this closet, fifteen years ago. The exciting times when he included her in his business and took her to Las Vegas, Nassau, and Mexico, came to mind. She ran her hand over the dress she wore to see Sinatra and the Rat Pack, the one she wore when he made the killing at the blackjack table and the little black number she wore the night Cher stopped by their table to comment on how much David resembled Elvis, especially from her stage vantage. Dicey recalled the terrible fight they had on their last night together after returning from Mexico City when she refused to take these things home with her to Delaware.

He was always frustrated by her refusal to take anything from him.

"These things are part of your territory, not mine. They stay here." Dicey insisted. This closet defined her to him. As much as she integrated into his life at times; she and David were always waiting for the next hand to be dealt. They were players on opposite sides of the table. She promised herself to sort through these things and send the most dated pieces to Goodwill—memories or not.

Her call to Dr. Drysdale that evening was reassuring. David had made some progress in the first 24 hours and although his vitals were still good, the swelling had not gone down. "We are really not expecting too much before 48 hours. However he is no longer on life support. The respirator has been removed; he is breathing on his own. That is progress"

"Dr. Drysdale, if the tumor is benign, why does David need an oncologist? Did a biopsy confirm the tumor removed yesterday was not cancer?"

"The tumor was benign as you have been told."

"I don't understand. Are you still his doctor even though it was benign?"

He paused to carefully pick his words "I will continue to be his doctor. It is complicated, and would be best if you wait to let him explain."

It was confusing. The brain tumor was not cancer but an oncologist meant David was still facing cancer—but where, what kind? For the second night, she had restless sleep that left her with unsettled feelings.

She turned off the answering machine, knowing that this number was only known to David's clients. No bets would be taken until David was able to take them himself. The cell phone, which he purchased exclusively for his calls to her, sat on the night stand—lit and waiting for his call which would not come tonight. Her own cell phone was there, too—for Dr. Drysdale's or Jen's calls. Thus organized she passed her second night alone in David's apartment.

The next morning after a leisurely breakfast, she approached the closet and chose a new red print dress, which slid perfectly over her figure. The shoes were less than comfortable since she rarely wore heels. The lightweight black wool jacket complimented the dress perfectly, and the wig with heavy blond highlights solved the problem of doing her hair. Every time she wore it she considered having streaks put into her own chestnut hair but somehow never did. She put all her purse items in the large pouch bag. Her cell phone interrupted her preparations.

"Mom, are you coming to see us tomorrow? I assume you are still in Maryland." Jen's voice was welcome although it made her uneasy to be talking to her daughter and have the mirror reflect a woman she hardly knew and barely recognized.

"Yes, to both, Jen. I'll come up after breakfast. Will that work for you? What are the kids doing?"

"They are looking forward to seeing you. We will be here. What is the story on David?"

"Well, Honey. Yesterday they did surgery to remove a benign brain tumor. Now, he is in an induced coma. His vitals are good. I can come to Frederick. The doctor asked me to stay available until they wake him up."

"I'm not going to say anything about that. You know what I think. Just come on up and let's have lunch and dinner together. Will you stay overnight?"

"I doubt it. See you about eleven tomorrow. Tell everyone hello for me. I love you."

"Love you too, Mom."

Dicey headed for her first appointment, thinking how much she looked forward to seeing the kids tomorrow. Tomorrow—Dicey was looking forward to a new day.

Tike was waiting for her. He thought about asking her to join him for a drink or some lunch, but he knew better than to cross that line.

Dicey knew that although David was not with her, his strength and influence was protecting her every moment. The envelope was exchanged and slipped into the lining of the large purse. As she walked out of the restaurant, a cell phone was ringing. It was the one David bought her for his calls. The only calls it ever received were from his cell phone. For an instant, joy came to her thinking mistakenly that it would be him. *Oh my God. No one can call this phone but David! But it can't be.* Dicey's heart beat fast and a bead of sweat glistened on her lip. Her hand trembled as she held the phone and listened to the message going to voice mail.

"Hello, I am trying to locate a friend of a friend of mine. If you are Dicey, would you please call me back? My name is Suzette. Thank you."

Suzette? Dicey thought. *How did she get this number?* The fear and questions this brought to mind sapped all of Dicey's energy. *Why is she looking for me? Does she know Delores Grant is Dicey? No one, not even Jen, knows me by that name—only David.*

Dicey did not have the answers to the questions racing through her mind. She struggled with her composure and checked her watch. Her plan to have lunch at a favorite diner and make her second appointment needed to change. Instead, she headed back to the apartment to eat and restore her balance. As she approached her usual parking space, she saw Suzette entering the building. Her need to run to David was overwhelming, but she could not do that. Her home in Delaware popped into her mind along with a longing for it. Shaking her head to clear it of thoughts that would undermine her spirit, she turned into the parking lot and parked behind some trees in time to see David's girlfriend come from the building and leave in her car.

Should I go in? She wondered as she required her senses to support her practical mind. Since Suzette was just here, it was unlikely that she'd return immediately. Dicey decided to go in, pack her bag and leave for Jen's after the last collection. A quick call to her daughter alerted her to the change in plans.

Dicey entered the apartment and saw the note that had been slipped under the door.

> *Dicey, it is very important to talk to you. Please call me. 410 555-0979. David has given me a message for you. Suzette.*

The note was alarming, on so many levels. Years of association with David had conditioned her to think as he would. His suspicious and cautious nature seemed to infuse her. Dicey became like David. She would increase her odds against Suzette. Neither her face nor actions would give Suzette any clues. There must be a reason for the lie that David had sent her; it was baiting, but she did not know why. *Whatever she wants, she will have to get from David—not me.* The woman who had never set in a poker game began to act like a gambler with a winning hand that needed to be protected. She copied the note and replaced it on the floor. Since her anonymity and the apartment had been compromised, she would vacate the premises. As she packed her bag, she made decisions on what must be done before she left. She cleared out any traces that she had been there: trash was tied up and put in the suitcase with her clothing; the bathroom was cleaned; fresh linens were put on her bed and the wrinkled ones were also packed in her bag; the refrigerator was checked for hints of her stay; the television was tuned to ESPN before turning off again with the remote. She had done everything she could think of and was looking back over the space when she thought of the safe. If there was a possibility the apartment could be entered, the safe would be vulnerable. Dicey did the only thing she could do—she opened the safe and took the money David handed her in the hospital as well as the significant amount that was already there. A large envelope marked *important papers* emerged under the cash. She took the envelope, shut the door, and spun the combination lock. The money and important papers went in the Coach bag; she headed for her 2:30 appointment with Tommy G. Dicey went down to the basement, followed the corridor around to the adjoining building and exited a far entrance, walked behind the trees and got into her car. She was afraid to look at the entrance to the apartment. What would she do if she saw Suzette? Slowly she raised her eyes. The walk was empty. She drew the first full breath since closing the safe.

When Dicey got to the mall she pulled into the parking garage next to Nordstrom's and stashed the money in the tire well in the floor of her SUV. Large bills in bundles were pushed around the tire and between the spokes of the rim. The well clicked shut and she sighed in relief, smiling at the crazy, unlikely task just finished. *The last thing in need now is a flat tire.*

Dicey walked, clutching her bag as if it had some special security significance to her mission. It did not, except giving her something to hold onto. Tommy was at the fountain in front of the Cinema. He handed her the envelope, said not a word and walked to a large black Cadillac with District of Columbia Congressional tags. Dicey did the luckiest thing she had done all day. She called Marquette and said she had to change the time and place for their meeting. Little did she know that keeping her appointment at his office would have given Suzette another opportunity to intercept her.

"Hello, this is Dicey. Can I see you at 3:10? I have an appointment later this afternoon."

"Of course, Dicey. Where?"

"Cherry Tree Shopping Center. You know where that is? I'll be in front of Dunkin Donuts. I am on my way there now."

"That will work for me."

*   *   *

Marquette did not have to wait for Dicey, but arrived only moments ahead of her. His mature eye admired her as soon as he saw her. What a shame this lovely lady was one of David's. Somehow the red dress and shoes did not fit her; she seemed to be costumed. At another time or place he would make a move to make conversation and maybe a connection. Besides being older than he would expect of one of David's women, she had a class that belied today's mission and meeting. Her smile was forced and Marquette saw apprehension in her eyes. Her nervous hand took his prepared envelope and tried to stash it into her purse, dropping everything. As the purse and its contents hit the cement, the events of the day seemed to crash around

Dicey and her composure melted. She froze with her arms rigid to her sides.

Jacques Marquette knew in an instant that she was upset beyond dropping her keys, the envelope and purse.

"Let me . . ." She allowed him to gather everything.

"Thank you," she smiled and shrugged the clumsy scene.

Her distress, although momentary, touched him and his instinct was to offer some kind of aide. He wanted to do more than pick up the dropped items but he dared not be too forward. The lawyer reached into his pocket and handed her his card.

"Dicey, my card. David knows he can depend on me, and I'm available if you need anything." He said with a warm southern accent that she figured was South Carolina. Jacques Marquette's smile was warm and somehow comforting to the lady trying to hold everything together. This man was definitely different from the other two clients she met. He did not fit the stereotype for most of David's associates—any more than she did

Dicey left the meeting running his name through her mind. *Jacques Marquette.*

*　　*　　*

It had not been a good day for the overwrought Suzette. Her calls to the person, Dicey, were not returned. She found David's apartment but not the woman. Now, Suzette was parked outside the Professional Building on Rock Creek Parkway at the intersection with New Hampshire Avenue. The fancy brick and brass sign announced the law offices of Horton, Horton and Marquette. She expected the woman, Dicey, to meet with Jacques Marquette after work hours, like Luke Horton said. She had been there since 4:45. It was nearing 7:00 and her patience was wearing thin. Not one woman had approached the law offices. She left when the lawyers and office staff headed for the Capitol Beltway for the weekend. The only car in the parking lot was hers. She put it in gear and sped out, gripping the steering wheel with frustration and attitude.

*　　*　　*

David loved Patti and little Patrick. He agonized over the divorce that ended the marriage, which seemed like a wonderful adventure when he and Patti were young. He faced his past choices and saw Patti's sad face. She simply could not live with a man who did not bring home a check after working nine to five. David could not work for anyone, punch a time clock, or ignore the thrill of beating the odds and making a bankroll on chance. Patti could not be excited when he brought home more than enough, nor could she believe, when he brought home nothing, that the money would roll again soon. She could not live with a man who would make a living outside the law. David understood and let her go but it meant he had to let Patrick go, too. He would do everything he could to make sure the boy had all he needed and he would have his mother to make his life complete. The man simply did not know that a boy could be just as lost without a father.

Now there was total freedom to be what he wanted to be, in a world most would never know. There was not any guilt in the choice he and Patti made, it was best for everyone. The divorce would protect his wife and son from the harsh reality of the street life he had chosen.

David eased into the gambling world without pretending he had another occupation, without trying to live in the bounds and obligations of marriage and family. Word filtered back through the grapevine to his hometown and to Dicey. She was probably the only one in the entire network of family, friends and classmates that was not saying, "I can't believe it."

Making book is a street life and anyone choosing to do it had better be street savvy, and more than that, had better know how to survive in the most primal way. While building a clientele, the bookie had to build a reputation for not only paying his losses but collecting his wins. One was as important as the other. David started at the gym to improve his stature and muscles. While in the Army he had been an MP; he knew how to strong arm and how to subdue those who resisted him. Secretly he looked forward to the resister and relished the power it would take to show who was in charge. That was the best part of his military career. At the gym, it did not take him long to call those muscles and that brute force back into his life. While watching <u>The Godfather</u>, David reached two major decisions: he would not subject his family to his life of crime and he would maintain a certain level of class. He needed to arm himself so after buying a gun, he went to New York and bought the finest suits, shirts, ties and shoes he could afford.

Delores was changing Jen's diaper and pretty strung out on domestic demands when he called. Today was not a good day for David to wrinkle her life. Josh had the chicken pox and she was getting through the day after two hours of sleep. David only wanted a small piece of her but she had no pieces to spare. His talk of gambling, betting, horses, games and large amounts of money seemed so trivial; she could not get her mind around it. All she could do was assure him of her strange sort of love and hope he knew what he was doing. David kept talking about geography and she tried to pay attention to his thinking. It may be true that this was all legal in Nevada but he lived in Maryland. It may be a matter of geography, but geography mattered.

She suggested he move to Las Vegas. His laughter came across the telephone as he said, "I am leaving tomorrow," and settled down to tell her. A job at the Lucky Charm sounded like a wonderful, colorful, exciting world as she wiped sticky fingers and tabletop. He talked vividly of it, but to Dicey, it was way too far from her reality of obligations and responsibility. This would be a separation of their lives. David could deal cards or whatever people did in Las Vegas but she could not see herself clear to encourage or even care if it was his big chance.

"Dicey, I am only telling you this so you won't hear it from some grapevine." Her interest in his life and choices had never been so low. The crying baby, covered with itchy spots and dishes in the sink kept her from contemplating his bright lights and celebrity elbows in Las Vegas.

"Now I will worry about you. That is new; I never worried about you before. I may even say a prayer for you."

"Prayers are good. Don't worry, Dicey. I can take care of myself. Do you need anything? I am more than flush."

"Save it for a rainy day. You can't win every time."

"You are there in Delaware, having babies and that is more risky than what I have decided to do." At that moment, he was more than funny, he was probably right. After hanging up the phone, she realized he had not asked how she was doing or what might be happening in her life. This was another one of David's efforts to get approval for something he knew his mother would not like. She resented the call from this motherless man when she had her hands full with children that were children. Her compassion was thin and she felt a great loss as if someone had died.

CHAPTER 5

Suzette understood magnetism and his was pure and potent; David was everything she wanted in a man, handsome, strong, exciting and older. The romantic vision of the ideal was not hers; had never been. Romance was way overrated. Security, comfort and satisfaction were the important things in life. Suzette found all these in David, especially security. Satisfaction was a bonus.

She was unlike anything he had ever desired. Her animal appetite was cloaked in an unexpected brilliant mind. She was a beautiful and sexy partner. At the end of the day, good sex was the reward he claimed. He drew her to him like raking in the pot from the center of the table; he was satisfied. After long lists of conquests, they both found a relationship that required no yielding. The ease of it was the death of it.

The relationship and lavish lifestyle he provided made her happier than she had ever been. No doubt he admired her beauty but made no concession to it. There was little doubt that if asked what was the most important part of their relationship they would both would reply—sex and security. Life was interesting and pleasant in their home in the Watergate condominiums along the Potomac. Each spent time apart, never questioning the other. She liked stepping on the elevator with important politicians and celebrities who were on stage at the Capitol or the Kennedy Center for the Performing Arts. David liked that too, and with tongue in cheek, smiled at them with his Elvis-like sneer. He knew which of the 'high and mighty' would be calling him about the sweet sixteen in the March Madness NCAA tournament, which would need to talk to him about the NBA game in Houston, and which was hung up on their home team regardless of their record or hopes of winning. He especially liked stupid, rich gamblers. Washington was a city with more than one truth, more than one level of life, and a very dirty underground. Suzette was not happy that he would not socialize with his neighbors but he was adamant. The people that she saw as friendly celebrities, he saw as clients. He did not socialize with clients.

David was not a man of intellect, but he admired that in his lover. Except for Suzette, the women in his life were dumb, plain, and simple. Suzette was different and he was amazed that someone so smart would chose to be with him. She traveled in her job for the State Department and always looked forward to coming home to this place with this man who was entirely different from the men who constantly hit on her. Suzette wore a wedding band on her left hand/third finger when she was away from Washington. Sometimes that helped, but being married did not ward off the wolves, a circumstance that seemed to exist in every corner of the globe. And, she did not always turn the hungry men away. Ironically, it was a wolf that rescued her from the corner where her family lived in beautiful poverty, the only way to describe Haiti. Even in her dirty hovel, with ill-fitting clothes, her rescuer saw something in the cowering, dirty young girl. He marveled at her beauty and took her home to a new life, taught her social graces, educated her at Georgetown University, and finally set her loose by his untimely death. Suzette expected to be in his will but everything went to the children she had never met and he hardly saw during their lives. Although she was bitter about being left out of his will, she mourned him like a father and moved on taking with her an important lesson about counting on a man. It was years and many relationships later that she met David and found the security she lost with the death of her benefactor. It was a bonus that she genuinely liked him. Most of all, he gave her a safe place to enjoy a bountiful life full of the finer things. This savvy lady had been stashing her income for three years but she wanted more—much more than she could earn or save. Now David was sick and if he died, she wanted the money she knew he had. Suzette wondered how she could be sure the wealth she felt entitled to would someday be hers. He had a son and although he told her he would take care of her, she had never seen a will. Blood was thicker than water and surely thicker than sex and security. The collections he made during the past week brought him one of the biggest bankrolls of his career. He had dreamed of a big score before retiring and so he took deep bets. The insiders were assuring that, with an upset at

Wimbledon, David would collect instead of paying. She recalled that the morning he told her of his good fortune was the same day that the doctor called to tell David about the brain tumor. Neither David nor Suzette knew the great sums had come to the man in time to pay huge medical bills instead of funding a grand life. The situation with his health and the induced coma made it imperative that she insure her own future—she was not going to lose what she needed if David died. There would not be false hopes to be in his will; she would do what she needed to do to have control of his money while he was sick . . . . and if he recovered, well, everything could be as it was . . . maybe.

In this urban life and with great concentration, she kept her tribal roots subdued but tonight in the dark bedroom alone in the luxury apartment with the lights along the Potomac ignored, her native side compelled her back to her hot, island village where a glimpse of the past and future mesmerized the woman. She saw her mother smoking a hallucinogenic drug and letting her eyes float to the back of her brain. She listened again to her mother's voice—soft like a misty rain, which takes the temperature down two degrees and raises the humidity until breathing is almost impossible. The young girl stepped close again to hear the words, which her mother had promised were only for her. "Good bye, Suzette. You are lost to me; your face will be only a memory. Watch out for snakes . . . no wait . . ." The old woman took a deep breath and looked deeper into the kaleidoscope fog, ". . . watch out for snake eyes." Why had this old image, which had been suppressed for years come to haunt her tonight? She used every trick to deny her mother and seek a new glimpse into the future. Another image came scaring and compelling—she saw David dead.

It was risky. David would not be forgiving if he knew what she planned, but she had to chance it. He had been very secretive but she knew two things: he had a mysterious friend named Dicey, and he had a covert apartment. Two things she had hints about but had not been important to her before. Never before did she care about David's women or where he went to be with them. To get her hands on the money she knew David had stashed, she would have to find both. She went to his desk, forced the lock to search through his papers where she found a utility bill with the address she was seeking. With that in her purse, she headed to the hospital to wait during his surgery and get her hands on David's cell phone, which the nurse, happily, obliging, handed over to her. She smiled at her good luck to have, in hand, two things David had so carefully kept from her. She called Lucas Horton of Horton, Horton & Marquette; he would help her. "Luke, Suzette."

He knew it was she as soon as she spoke his name in her strong, French, island accent; his heart leapt at the sound. His torch was long burning and hot, but not hot enough to ignore David King's importance in her life. She knew of his yearning for her—as women do when a man stays on the safe side of passion. It was a knowledge she saved for a time like this.

"I need some help. David is in the hospital and may die. I need to be sure this person, Dicey, is not moving in while he is ill. I am afraid that she will walk away with everything if David dies? I don't know her real name but David calls her Dicey."

"What do you want me to do?"

"Jacques Marquette is a client of David's. He might know something about a woman called, Dicey. I need to find her." He wondered why she did not call Marquette herself but was happy she had called him.

"I am sorry to hear David is ill. I'll see what Jacques knows?"

"Thanks Luke. Just be very careful about it. Don't let Jacques know you are asking for me. Call if you get anything and we will meet for a drink." This was his first chance to be alone with the intriguing, beautiful woman. His hopes soared that this could be more than a drink date—maybe the start of something big. He would use his best lawyer technique to secure some information and get into Suzette's debt and maybe her pants, too.

Luke Horton set about making small talk with his partner about the bets placed last week on Wimbledon and the NBA championship game. He had no luck in bringing the small talk around to personal inquiries about David King. Just as he was about to give up, Marquette announced he would close the office tonight because he was meeting someone at 5:30. That was highly unusual.

"You are working late . . . on a Friday night?"

"Not working, paying off last week's bet on Wimbledon. If you want to bet on a sure thing, bet on my six o'clock martini."

Luke Horton had earned his opportunity with Suzette. He was more than excited when he told her David's emissary would be coming to Marquette's office at 5:30. He heard her release a breath, as if she'd been holding it. "I owe you, Luke." Luke smiled. He was counting on that.

CHAPTER 6

Delores was happy to be visiting her family and the joy of the children held at bay the events of the day.

Jen was waiting to get her mother alone to talk to her about the things that were filling her days while helping David. Delores was prepared and resolved to be as honest as she could.

Jen poured coffee and shooed the children off to watch television. The time had come for her mother to explain and for her to understand as best she could.

"Mom, I need to know what is going on with you and David."

"I know you do, dear. I don't know all the answers because David was unable to talk to me before he had the surgery and went into the coma. It has been two days and I don't know any more than I did when I talked to you. He asked me to stay here while he is comatose, and he has made his assets available to me to pay the hospital. He doesn't have insurance and the hospital needed to know the bills would be paid. I cannot imagine what four or more days in intensive care will cost." She decided not to mention the three collections she made this afternoon.

"It will take a lot of money."

"I know."

"Where is the money to pay his bills?" Now they were in territory that would upset Jen. Delores thought carefully before replying. To refuse to answer would cause as much worry as the truth.

"Right now, it is in the wheel well of my SUV."

"Mom! How much money is in the wheel well of your car?"

"I don't know, Sweetie. I didn't count it." To say that Jen went off the deep end would be an understatement. She began walking around the room, rubbing her forehead and twisting her hands. Delores went to her daughter, who threw her arms around her diminutive mother. "Jen, let's talk about it. I need some advice and have no one to turn to. This has gotten to be more than I expected and I am sure more than David expected. The complicating factor is the woman he lives with is doing some strange things. Before he went into surgery he asked me to do everything possible to avoid her, and now she's trying to reach me. I don't know how she got my cell number or how she found the apartment, but she did. David expected me to put his money in the safe at the apartment but after she located it, I couldn't do that. I know he doesn't trust her. I doubt she is concerned about his hospital bill. So . . . that is why I have the money in my car."

"Think, Mom. Is there anyone that David would trust to relieve you of this burden? I won't let you go on with this. If it is a lot of money . . . people do crazy things for money." A quiet fell over the mother and daughter as each was lost in thoughts about the situation. Delores had a feeling of relief that she was not alone in this mess, although she hated causing her daughter to worry since her first phone call two days ago. Their separate revelries were interrupted by Delores's cell phone bringing a call from Dr. Drysdale.

"Ms Grant, we are going to bring Mr. King out of his coma for a while in the morning. We usually have a family member standing by. I thought you were the person who should be here. It is most likely that he will be re-sedated to the coma level after we check his sight and some other factors. Can you be here at 9:00?

"Yes, Doctor. I will be there." Before hanging up she thought of a question to ask the doctor. "Tell me, Dr. Drysdale, is it possible to get and pay Mr. King's partial bill tomorrow when I am there?" It was an unusual question.

"I will notify the business office by e-mail and we will see if we get a reply in the morning. I am not sure what can be accomplished on Saturday but we will try. If not Saturday—Monday for sure. The hospital is always happy to be paid." The call was finished.

Jen brought a new reality to the situation—her mother could not walk into the hospital with thousands and thousands of dollars in cash. "Just how are you going to pay them, Mom? Maybe a wheelbarrow and shovel?" They both laughed at this humor that was the younger woman's hallmark. But, it was still a serious situation and they were back to thinking who could help. Delores thrust her hand into her pocket as if reaching deep for answers. Her fingers felt something. She did not remember what or when a ticket or card had been put in the pocket of her dress. With great curiosity she drew it out and read, *Jacques L. Marquette, Esquire.—Lawyer.* Delores did not believe in coincidence; she believed in providence. The feeling of trust she had when she met him just hours ago came back to her. She would not have to discuss where she got David's money; he would know the source. Almost without thinking, she decided this man would be the one who could help. She only had her gut feelings to go on.

It was 9:30, much too late to intrude on a virtual stranger. She would call him tomorrow and hope that Saturdays were not sacred to a partner in the firm of Horton, Horton & Marquette, PA. Surprisingly, her rest was sound and refreshing, maybe because she was in the home of her most beloved, maybe because David would be out of the coma for a little while in the morning, maybe because she had a course of action for tomorrow or maybe because she was simply exhausted. Whatever the reason, she was grateful to rise early and renewed.

Jen was happy to see her mother looking so lively and lovely as she provided coffee and quiche before sending her off to the hospital. "I will call you later."

"Are you coming back?"

"Yes, dear . . . if I don't run away to Delaware."

"That is the best idea yet, Mom!"

But, Delores (Dicey) Grant was not going to leave David.

*   *   *

The trip they made to Las Vegas was in the heyday of the strip, when men wore ties and the ladies were dressed to the nines. There was exclusiveness to gambling and a gentlemanly way to enjoy the games. The slot machines were one arm bandits, nothing digital. Cherries and sevens reigned supreme. The dealers at the tables were skilled professionals and if they were beautiful—all the better. Tips were generous and winners and losers blended together. Celebrities wanted to mix with the customers and recognize the regulars. David wanted Dicey to see it; he wanted to give it to her and show his appreciation for all she had done for him. As soon as he was recovered from his heart surgery, he began to plan the trip, refusing to accept her first refusal to go. He changed his tactic and convinced her that the only way he could go was to have her with him. The doctor's would not condone him traveling alone. It was a smart move. "I need you to go with me and if you do not go; I **will** go alone—damn the doctors!"

She relented and even got excited to see this place in the desert where Dean Martin and Frank Sinatra were royalty.

"I promise you will love it Dicey, and besides, everything we do there will be legal. As I said, it is all a matter of geography. All you have to do is relax and enjoy yourself."

It was the most wonderful time she had had since she was widowed. The time for David was special too. He had his Dicey in his world, and it was like a trip to never-land because he knew he could not and would not be able to hold her there. During the time she was tending his recovery, David had his first romantic notions toward her He began to feel a new kind of love. It was no longer the childlike profession that did not want or need commitment. Was it possible that he could want her to leave her undefined role and become his partner in passion? After all these years a chemistry that he could not deny was consuming him. Her touch and her smile did strange things to the man. The realization that his recovery meant she would be leaving, left him weak. On the last night before she was returning to Delaware, David called her to sit with him on the sofa. "Dicey, I love you."

"I know, David. I love you, too."

It was the old refrain they had said for years. She kissed him softly on the lips as she had done many times before except this time his arms did not let her go. His inner being and body stirred; he wanted her.

"Dice. I am asking you to stay with me. Don't go back to Delaware. Live with me here or in DC. It doesn't matter as long as we are together. I want you to come to my bed."

Surprised by his kiss and arms, circling her body holding her to his chest, she looked into his eyes, saw his longing, and started to cry. There was no movement to draw away as she slowly shook her head from side to side.

"I am still in love with Greg. It may be hard to believe after two years, but it is true. I don't know how my love for you fits into the picture now that he is gone, but it has been there all the years—while he was here. David, I can't be with you every day and I don't need to be in your bed." Her hand traced his chin and followed down his neck as he leaned into her touch.

"Haven't we always loved each other?"

"*Yes and it cannot change now while I am still grieving. If we go in there and make love, I will lose something else and I cannot afford another loss. Does any of this make sense?*"

"*Dicey . . .*" The man who seldom asked for anything and never asked twice, with her name and emotion in his voice, begged for what he wanted. "*Dicey . . . .*"

"*I can't.*"

David looked at her as if he had never seen her before. She was not the woman he had known since childhood, nor the woman he took for granted, nor the woman who challenged his world. Dicey was a beautiful newly revealed love and she was saying—no. He bent his forehead to touch hers, and shed a quiet tear with her. He did not understand.

CHAPTER 7

As she drove in to meet Dr. Drysdale at David's bedside, she debated with herself on the propriety of calling Jacques Marquette so early. She decided to call at the last possible moment before walking into the hospital.

Marquette was surprised and delighted to have a call from Dicey wake him on Saturday morning. Whatever the reason, he wanted her call.

"I hope I am not calling too early. This is Dicey."

He sat straight up in bed to gather his thoughts. It was early for him but that did not matter. He had not expected to hear from the intriguing lady in red that had stayed in his mind since yesterday afternoon. His hesitation caused Dicey to back pedal.

"I'm sorry; I shouldn't be bothering you. Please accept my apology. Good-bye."

"No. No. Dicey, I want to talk to you."

"Mr. Marquette, I hope you are sincere in your offer to help me. I need advice and I am not sure if it is legal advice . . ."

"Please, call me Jacques. Of course I will help, if I can."

"Thank you."

She is upset, he thought as she thanked him again. He could tell she was unsure of him but he knew, no matter what her problem was, her trust was not misplaced. They arranged to meet for lunch at noon.

She snapped the phone closed and went into the hospital. The old feelings of apprehension came over Dicey as she followed the familiar corridor to the intensive care unit to be greeted by Dr. Drysdale, who introduced her to the other doctors in attendance. Being mindful of her concern for the patient, he stepped aside so she could approach the bedside and speak to David in soft tones.

He looked so good, so restful and the reclining position drew the age wrinkles from his face. She had never seen him so peaceful and

45

handsome and she could not help but wonder if his usual hard-aged look was due to the lifestyle he engaged in more than the years turned on the calendar. "I am waiting for you, David," she whispered and stepped back so the medical team could begin their work.

"Ms. Grant if you will wait in the hall, we will call you in when he is awake. It is important to have a familiar voice for the patient as he comes from the coma. We believe his hearing is restored but we don't know about his sight. He may be agitated. It is quite expected. You can come in when we have him settled for the testing. Give us some time; this procedure will take less than twenty minutes."

Dicey walked to the corridor, and looked back at David through a plate glass wall. It was the longest twenty minutes she could remember; just watching the clock slowly approach 9:10, 9:20, 9:35

Dr. Drysdale came out and took her hand. "Mr. King is awake and asking for you. Let me prepare you. His vision has not returned. We have tried to assure him that there is improvement in the swelling and there will be more, but he is frightened and being uncooperative. We could sedate him right now, but I think you could help him settle. We would like to have him awake for at least ten more minutes. Are you up to it?"

"Doctor, tell me the truth; I will not lie to David. Is his sight lost?"

This woman was more amazing than he realized. Her command of the situation and strong desire to act positively were not expected in situations like this when most loved ones wanted the softest route. He took a moment to fully brief her on the condition of David's brain at the site of the tumor.

"The tumor was successfully removed. The swelling has begun to recede. Hearing returns first then sight. We told him it was too soon to know the outcome on that. Mr. King knew at the onset that he would most likely not see at this juncture but patients forget what they have been told. They want to see—understandably."

When he finished, she stood, straightened her sweater, and took her first step to carry this news to David.

"David. I am here." She laid her hand on his chest and bent to kiss him in the familiar fashion of their life.

"Dice. Dice." He said, his voice dry, raspy. "Don't go away."

He could not hold on to her, but she knew his need and held him with a half hug that could only circle to the bed, her elbows tight to his waist and her hands under his shoulders. He took her in as if he were swaddled in her care and repeated her name. She could feel him try to rise up and then yield to her caress.

"David, listen to me. I only have a few minutes before you will go to sleep again. The doctors are running some tests on you while I am with you and then it will be two more days before you will see me again, and you *will* see me then." She kissed his cheek. "Hey, you have gotten this far. I trust your doctors, and I will not lie to you. You know that. This is day three since the removal of the tumor, which was benign as they expected. They do not know if your sight will come back, but there is no reason to believe it won't. Your hearing obviously has returned and that is how it goes; the hearing returns first, then the sight. Stay calm while they are testing. I will be here until you go to sleep again."

"Stay," he pleaded. His hands tightened on her, as if he could hold her there.

She smiled and shook her head, forgetting for the moment that he could not see. "You have been dealt a good hand, three of a kind. Now it is time to draw two and wait for the cards to show. You know the odds are good that your three of a kind will hold against the table." She continued talking about things that meant something to him until Dr. Drysdale gave her a thumbs up sign.

David began to drift away. "I love . . ."

She knew what he was saying and heard all three words.

"You did a good job for us, Ms. Grant. We have some very encouraging data. I hope this was not too hard on you because you were a big help." She rose to shake his hand. "Care for a cup of coffee?"

Delores spent a pleasant few minutes with Dr. Drysdale, enjoying the invigorating infusion of caffeine as the morning sunlight poured into the hospital café. They did not talk of David, but addressed the question she had asked yesterday.

"The business office will have Mr. King's bill ready on Monday," Dr. Drysdale said. "They couldn't have it for you today. I will call you on Monday or Tuesday when the team makes the decision to end the coma. Meanwhile, you know you can visit him anytime around the clock. By his request you are the only visitor allowed, now that his son has left."

"Yes, thank you." She needed a few minutes alone to sort her feelings after being with David, awake, but lying helpless and blind in the bed upstairs. Dicey questioned her own strength and refused to imagine that his sight would not be restored. David would never be able to adjust to blindness; she knew him too well. Something deep inside told her she would hate being tied to him because of this. It was a reality which unnerved her. When Greg faced life changing health issues, she had not hesitated to rush in with him. Dicey knew her love for her husband had always been different from her caring for David but until this doubting moment, she did not realize the degree of difference. The alliance between lifetime friends had not tied their lives together since she was widowed. How could such a tragic thing cause a union that love and time had not been able to cement. But, it was there and she knew, as she knew her next breath would be drawn and exhaled, the truth. Dicey was David's in time of need, yet she could not contemplate the possibility of an overwhelming need that could take the rest of her life to fulfill.

*　　*　　*

Jacques Marquette sat in his sports car in the parking lot of Santo's Greek Restaurant., watching Dicey drive in and look around before leaving her car. She looked different. Her hair was darker without streaks. *She wore a wig yesterday*, he thought. Now her natural locks were loosely blowing in the breeze. He liked it, and the casual sport clothes opposed to the red dress and heels of yesterday. *Lovely!*

He was even happier to see her, if possible. His professional ability to access a person on outward appearance had served him well preparing for court and he saw something in this woman that he had not seen yesterday. She had some concerns behind her smile that were shading and tempering her demeanor. They went to a quiet table, which was hidden, by a short wall and green plants. He knew this table and had used it many times before.

"Dicey, may I choose a wine for you? If you will take my suggestion of the flounder almandine, I know the perfect one." So far, she had needed only to nod her head and he allowed her to stay in her quiet place while he conferred with the waiter. Then he waited for her and noticed that the silence between them was not at all awkward, but more of a probing, searching time to see how they fit together. When she finally looked into his eyes, she saw an interest that had not been projected to her, by anyone, for over seventeen years. Jacques did not turn from her gaze, instead he held it.

The wine was poured, and the sommelier gone before she spoke to him.

"Jacques, this wine and a nice lunch seems a blessing to me," she said as she lifted her glass as a toast. "Thank you."

He let the wine and food mellow the tension in the woman and did not venture to ask any of the questions that were shouting in his brain. *Am I infatuated?* He wanted to know her relationship to David King. *Are they lovers?* He wanted to know if his pounding feelings had to be suppressed. She did seem to relax, and her smile became easy and generous until he felt comfortable offering the help she said she needed.

"Are you alright, Dicey? Your call this morning seemed distressed. Is there anything I can do for you? Professionally? Personally?" he added to let her know he was open for more, welcomed it even. His gaze stayed locked on hers.

"I have to trust someone." Her own words, admitting that she was lost, brought tears to her eyes. She reached for a tissue saying, "If I am making a mistake . . ."

Jacques reached across the table, took the tissue from her and offered his pleasantly man-scented handkerchief. "Dicey, look at me. I am here because I want to help you. You can trust me, I promise. Are you in legal trouble?"

"No. I don't think I am in that kind of trouble. I just don't know which way to turn. David is in a tenuous place. It will be two days before we know if he will have his sight after his surgery. Before I go any further, I need to know how well you know David King. Be frank with me; do you think he would trust you?"

"Well, I know he is a reliable bookie and I make bets with him on a regular basis. We sometimes share a drink and argue about religion and politics, almost like a sport. He is a very likeable person and more complex than most people realize. I don't know much about his personal life. I do know he keeps a low profile, and the authorities are not too interested in him, as he stays clear of the drug world where the police concentrate. He is a strong and honest man. He said he doesn't socialize with his customers, but we share a meal occasionally. I believe he trusts me."

"I have known David all of my life. We have been close even though we have led separate lives," Dicey said, reassured by his description. "At times, especially when he has serious health issues, I have been very involved in his life. We are everything to each other, but we are not a couple. I know that is hard to understand."

It *was* hard for Jacques to understand, but such good news. He exhaled and drew a breath, as if new fresh air was filling his lungs. His spirits rose along with his hopes. Jacques was becoming a dreamer, and he wanted this woman, though *how* was still undefined. He faced the feelings that had been panging him since yesterday; he was smitten by a woman near his age, not ten to twenty years his junior. He smiled.

"Does my story strike you amusing?" Misreading his expression and suddenly confused and needing to be honest and clear on this man who was asking for her trust.

Jacques took her hand. "Dicey, I am smiling because I am happy that you and David are not a couple. I would have called *you* this morning if I had known that earlier." He smiled, squeezed her hand, released it, and ordered another glass of wine. "Let's talk about your problem and then, we can get on with getting to know each other." He had said exactly the right thing, comforting her. She wanted to like him.

She told him of David's coma and the money that she had in her possession. In a short time, he was aware of the need to pay the hospital with David's money and the attempt by Suzette to get her hands on it. They both laughed at the impossible scenario of her walking into the Greater Laurel-Beltsville hospital with thousands of dollars in cash. Jacques suggested an escrow account, which he would set up to pay the hospital. He would forward 20% to IRS as soon as David could tell them if he had or had not already done so. It was obvious that the collections that Dicey made were not submitted for taxes. She did know that Dave had an accountant and was sure he always paid his taxes; the only thing that could possibly land him in jail on a federal warrant. Jacques was relieved. He could not help her with this unless all taxes were paid. She had a fleeting fear that David might not approve of bringing Jacques into his business, but she was realist enough to know she could not protect his interest and her identity from Suzette if, God forbid, David should die. The comfort she felt with Jacques Marquette set her resolve that David would just have to accept her decision to trust this man.

"Let's enjoy our lunch now and while we eat, I would like to know more about you."

"My name is Delores Grant," she began, realizing that he only knew her by her nickname. Being with this man caused the woman to think about herself in terms she had denied for almost two decades. She was lonely and she had wanted to sit, talk, and reveal herself to a man who might find important the smallest details of her being. Her hopes of finding s man to fill a deep empty space had dwindled and she had stopped seeking him, not that the dark place had diminished, in fact, it had grown unrelentingly year after year. Sitting here in this restaurant, warmed by wine and a gallant smile, she wanted a man again. She wanted, and she had not wanted anything for so long. An old, but new, sensation was traveling her body from head to toe. Was it possible that someone might want her again, might stir her desire, might want to give her more than he gets?

In the time it took to eat the fish and drink the second glass of wine, Jacques knew about her family, her home in Delaware and the difficult widowhood she had endured. He was interested in everything and she found telling her story cathartic. She could not remember anyone asking for such a long time. His questions about her happiness and interest were sincere and in two hours, he knew more about what made her tick than David—because he never asked. David did not know she loved gardening or that poetry reading and writing were her pastimes. David did not know she loved classical music as well as honky-tonk.

Jacques contemplated how he could take her to enjoy her interest at Kennedy Center concerts and a redneck bar that featured the honky-tonkiest music in Nashville. There were no questions about her relationship with David; he knew enough. They were not a couple, and although Jacques wondered what David would think about his interest in Dicey, it really had no relevance.

They left the restaurant and went to his office, which was empty on a Saturday afternoon. There they counted the money and put it in his safe until all $89,908.00 could be deposited on Monday. David's important papers were left there, too. Dicey felt lighter than the purse, dangling loosely from her shoulder.

"Dicey, here is a receipt, made out to David King, for the deposit and my usual retainer fee which I will take from these monies. This is necessary to legitimize this business transaction. I will itemize a bill for my time to do the banking on Monday. That will go against the retainer. I hope you understand this protects you as well as my firm. I will put a note in the folder about withholding taxes pending Mr. King's availability for consultation."

It seemed all too wonderful to have the burdens of the last three days handled in such a matter-of-fact business-like manner. She was confident that David's interests had been served as she extended her hand to thank Jacques.

"Shall I call you Delores or Dicey?" He asked as he took her hand.

Such a simple question and yet it stopped her in her tracks. She laid her other hand on the one Jacques held and said, "Dorrie. You can call me, Dorrie." She could not share *Dicey* with him; that was David's. Her husband had always called her Dorrie. It was time to hear it again.

Jacques stalled her leaving as long as he could. He made himself content with her going as they agreed to meet at 10:00 on Monday morning to do the banking. She was tired and looking forward to getting back to Jen's with the news that the money was no longer in the tire well.

Jacques stayed in the quiet office. He put on his favorite music by Debussy and leaned back in his chair to do some thinking. He wanted to concentrate on the woman and all the possibilities a relationship could present to him but his lawyer mind kept going to necessary arrangements that had to be accomplished for the tarnished money in his safe. He knew this would get very complicated if the man in the hospital did not survive. He also knew that Delores Grant had no legal right to hold possession of the money. She only had hearsay permission from David. For her sake, he took the money to his safe but he was not comfortable having it there. "Please God; don't let David King die before we get the money in the bank on Monday", the man who seldom prayed—prayed.

*   *   *

"Jen, Hi Honey. I will be heading back to Frederick in a couple of hours. The day went very well and the lawyer was so helpful. I will fill you in when I get there, but you will be glad to know that my wheel well is empty."

"That is good news. You sound so much better, Mom."

"I am. Hold me a bite to eat; I will be there by eight."

Dicey would go by the hospital first. Since she was the only allowed visitor, she could do some thinking at David's bedside. The room was quiet and David's steady breathing was the only sound except for the pulsing from the machines attached to him. There were so many things she wanted to tell him, but instead of saying a word, she let them run through her mind. The thing that struck her most was the desire to tell David about Jacques' kindness and the hope that he would approve of her trust in the lawyer. The only thing she said was, "David, you must get well. I need to talk to you and I need for you to talk to me."

Somewhere in his being, he knew she was with him and the Technicolor picture in his brain was far removed from the dark sightless time he had with her this morning. There was no doubt he wanted to be with her—if only he could break through the multicolored swirls between them.

It was late, at the end of a very long day, before Dorrie could think, uncluttered, about Jacques Marquette. She welcomed the familiar bed at her daughter's and stretched in the sheets that seemed to welcome new thoughts and fresh feelings. She cuddled in the cozy bed that seemed to be a part of a new comfort zone. She should be sleepy after the exhaustion of emotions at David's bedside and the excitement of being with Jacques . . . . basking in his attention. She was awake—or was she? She could see him clearly in the parking lot of Santo's with the sun on his blond hair that showed no signs of grey. His warm smile and green eyes were friendly and open. She could tell that his complexion needed sun protection or he would burn quickly. The wrinkles around his eyes were testimony of his quick-to-laugh disposition and his blond, full moustache seemed to provide staging for his light southern accent. All in all, she was full of pleasant thoughts of the ruggedly handsome Jacques Marquette. With these pleasant thoughts, she finally admitted sleep.

*　　*　　*

The first dizzy spell caused David to pull his car to the side of the road and it passed. The next day, he fell as he got out of bed and twice more during the day. Suzette was gone and that was good. The doctor did some initial examinations and sent him to a neurologist who ordered a MRI of his brain, a CAT scan, a PET scan and of course, blood work. The MRI showed a large tumor on the left-brain which was operable, but risky. Actually, David had no choice, if he wanted to function, the tumor had to be removed, malignant or benign. The PET scan did not show cancer cells in the tumor but something in the lungs caused the neurosurgeon to call Dr. Drysdale, an oncologist.

David had hardly digested the news of needing brain surgery when he got the news that the PET scan indicated cancer cells in the lungs. He was sure it was payment for the decades of smoking and being in smoke filled rooms. For many years, he had this gut feeling that someday a doctor would say, "There is a spot on your lung." Everyone has generic knowledge of chemo and radiation. Everyone knows the percentages on lung cancer and the average survival after a stage one diagnosis is three to eight years. But, this was not about everyone it was about David. After two biopsies, his doctor did not say, there is a spot on your lung. He said there are two spots, one on each lung and it is in stage four. There would not be three to eight years.

The odds were stacking against the gambler. The dealer could not be cursed; it was God. The man left the quiet of his luxury apartment and traveled to the secret one that he had shared with Dicey. He moved into the modest space and did some serious thinking. He had four days to get ready for the surgeon and the confinement afterward. For some reason the induced coma frightened him more than the surgery and the cancer. He would need Dicey while he was unconscious. He did not hesitate to have the surgery; it was necessary so he could fight the cancer. The slight chance that he would be blind after the surgery did not bother the gambler. When the doctor said a one in five chance to be left blind; he knew he would be fine. He had taken bets on those odds all his life. His will was reviewed, and a note was written to Suzette and placed in an envelope. He wanted her to know that he fulfilled his promise to her in his will, even though he knew even if cancer did not shorten his life, they would not be together much longer. Their relationship had run its course; he was

54

content to let her go. David organized his asset folder. All his stocks, bonds and accounts were in order in the envelope. Copies were made for his safe deposit box and the key was placed in the envelope with Dicey's name on it. He regretted leaving so much money in his safe but between doctor's appointments and collections, he had not had time to take care of it. She would take care of all these things as executor of his will if he died.

Who else but Dicey? The only condition she set when she agreed to be executor was assurance that she was not a beneficiary of anything named in it. He reluctantly agreed. She was adamant and stubborn about that, as she had been about any gift he had tried to give her through the years. Even in death, he would not be able to give her anything.

It took all four days to get everything in place before going into the hospital. He tried to call Dicey, and got her answering machine. He could not put all his news in a message on the machine. "Dice, I will call you in the morning. Please be there. Love ya."

She got her coffee and carried her phone to the porch the next morning and waited for his call. It was a good day to hear from David. She had been missing him and her life was feeling plain and flat. "Maybe David has something going that will include me," she thought. "I'd even be willing to go on vacation with him to some all-inclusive, pampering place. Something fun," she mused.

"Dicey, I am in the hospital and they are going to do surgery to remove a mass tomorrow. I know this is sudden, but can you come? Now?" She dropped everything and drove from Delaware, coming straight to the hospital. He sounded upset on the phone, so she did not press him for details. In truth, she was postponing getting the diagnosis. He could fill her in when she got there. However, time did not allow him to fill in the unknown spaces and she was again meshed in his life without quite knowing what was happening.

The note to Dicey took all day. He was not a writer; he did not know how to commit his thoughts and feelings to paper, but he struggled, he wrote, and he decided nothing would be erased or changed. Any word that went on the paper would be there for her to read. It would be as he felt it and as it poured forth. When it was finished, he read it once, folded it and took it to the safe along with other things he wanted her to handle—just in case . . . .

CHAPTER 8

Putting David's money safely in the bank was a significant event but by no means the most significant event in Dorrie and Jacques's day. As they were leaving the bank, he suggested a day at the Smithsonian and she readily agreed after calling Dr. Drysdale and learning that tomorrow would be the day David would be brought fully out of the coma. The scan this morning showed great improvement in the swelling. It was good news. She grasped it and agreed to Jacques plan to 'waste the day'.

As they walked from exhibit to exhibit, easily chatting about the wonders that were not new to them, yet were still amazing, he took her hand and easily claimed her space as his. Many discoveries were made of mutual likes and talk of things they would do together seeped into the day as easily as hunger for lunch seeped into their bodies. The dry sandwiches at the museum café were wonderful and the loud chatter of the people around them was background music.

"Jacques I feel like I played hooky from school or escaped from chores. Child-like pleasures."

Something special was happening; Dorrie could feel it—the magic of discovery, the joy of being with someone who fit so well into her day, the wonder of knowing it could happen again . . .

"I'd like to think we are running to something we don't want to miss." Jacques had his own take on the day.

What was it about new fascination that takes one back to their first teenage love? They were in a time out of time when anything was possible, everything was agreeable, and without exception, all was believable. If they had a question in their combined minds, it would be: Why not?

"We are not far from the Corcoran Art Gallery. Let's take a taxi there and close it this evening." Hand in hand, they walked through the gallery. It was late in the day and often they were the only ones in the galleries. The masterpieces were not new; the voyeurs had seen them all before, but something in their sharing brought new color, new discovery and new delight in each one. When she asked him to sit with her to enjoy the Renoirs, he remembered that he had always taken a seat in this gallery. Renoir's impressions were too overwhelming to walk past. She took in the pictures; he studied her. When they rose to leave, Dorrie reached for his hand.

The sun was setting when the taxi took them back to the lot at the Smithsonian to his car. "Dorrie," he began as they turned onto the Capitol Beltway, "we need some dinner. Hungry?"

"Famished." She always had her best appetite when she was happy.

"We could stop at a nice restaurant off New Hampshire Avenue or get some Chinese carry-out and eat at my home. It is up to you."

"Are you trying to get me alone at your place?" she laughed.

"Absolutely."

"I love Moo Goo Gai Pan."

Dorrie called Jen to tell her about her day and the good news from David's doctor. "I may not come to Frederick tonight. The lawyer and I are going to have dinner. I need to be at the hospital early tomorrow. I am fine. I'll call you."

Jen noticed the happiness in her mother's voice even though it had been a long time since she heard it.

Dorrie wondered at the sheer loveliness of the day, her happiness at being with him, although she did not know where they were going with today's feelings. Jacques occasional speculative glances at her told her he was wondering the same thing.

Jacques had his own musings. No past relationships were worth recalling. He had had his conquests but they were not unlike being serviced—no commitments and awkward mornings waiting for last night's partner to leave as soon as courtesy allowed. From what he had learned from Dorrie, she had not allowed a man to get close since her husband died, not even David.

At their age, *dating* was weird; *love* was undefined, and *sex*, well, it was not something that just happened. They were not wild young lovers who tore off their clothes and banged up against the foyer wall, but here was an undeniable fire consuming the loneliness and complacency that had reconciled their lives for many years.

Without being sure of the other, each contemplated new and exciting possibilities.

Moving along the busy beltway, they traveled further away from Laurel and the hospital. She allowed a thought about David and admitted to herself that she ran to him every time a suitor got to close. "David has been the only man in my life since Greg died, and as I said, we are not a couple." Hardly realizing she had spoken aloud, she surprised herself.

Her words and actions were opening the door for the gentleman, and he was not missing any clues. He was amazed how forthright—how candid she was.

While Jacques was contemplating how much future he could have with Dorrie; she was questioning if she had the courage to want Jacques, and there was a nagging feeling that she was somehow being disloyal to David. Although she did not say it, Dorrie thought what she had with David was the most she would ever have or want in her life.

They walked arm in arm into his house where he led her to the sofa, passed a pillow to the small of her back and went to the phone to order the food. She turned her attention to his very modern home, which was unlike her traditional choices but seemingly right for Jacques. The lines were sharp, the touches artistic and the colors warm. She liked it.

"Dinner will be here in about 30 minutes. I have poured a wine that goes well with nondescript food," he joked as he carried the wine and joined her on the sofa. They talked of their day in Washington and of the possibility of walking the Inner Harbor in Baltimore. Conversation was easy and plans crept in naturally. "Am I crazy or does it feel like we have known each other for a long time?" When she did not pull away or answer, he continued, "Because we are not youngsters, I feel we need to use our time together wisely, starting right now. I don't want to court you, try to impress you, or waste any time. Will you let me into your life? Are there any reasons why we can't start doing the things we know we both enjoy? Tomorrow and the next day? Together? Who knows, being a couple could be our future? There is only one way to find out." He was well aware that at their age, they did not have a lifetime ahead. However, he was cognizant that they would know how to use all the time they had. So much common ground had been found in one day, he would think in terms of acres and acres of time and space. He felt expanded.

"Jacques, I have not been in these waters before. This has been a wonderful day and the best part has been being with you." She tilted her head to his shoulder pausing to enjoy the moment. Her head rose and her eyes looked into his. "I understand how important time is to us. If I ask myself what I want right now, it is being here with you . . . yes, tonight and tomorrow. I come with a lot of baggage. We cannot ignore what brought us together in the first place." She did want to break the mood or even say *his* name. She did not want to think about blindness or cancer either.

Jacques, the lawyer, was listening very carefully to her words. First, he noticed that she did not qualify her words with *but.* That was good. She did not say *David.* That was very good. David was very much a part of what was happening here. He decided to help her by bringing David openly into the conversation. "Your life is in Delaware; that is the life I want to become part of. Your life is not here; it is not David. If it were David, you would be a couple and you would not be with me now." He placed his fingers over her mouth to stop the words she was about to say. "Wait, Dorrie. Let me say this." She returned his smile. "He has been your security blanket keeping you from reaching for your own happiness. I want to take the blanket away," he said firmly. "I want to be the man that makes you want more, or at least as much as you had before. I believe I can love you enough so you don't need David."

It was a pivotal moment. *Did I go too far?* He thought. Her wide-eyed look as she listened to his words frightened him. He drew her head back to his shoulder as an apology for being so blunt. Then he lifted her chin so her face could erase his fear.

She kissed him lightly. "I never thought I needed David, Jacques." Even as she said it, she knew it was true.

The doorbell interrupted. Jacques paid the delivery boy, put the food on the kitchen counter and returned to the sofa where she was waiting for him. Her smile warmed his heart and he knew that he had not gone too far in discounting the importance of her devotion to her friend. Jacques was confident David would not be able to keep him from Dorrie.

"I think we only have each other to consider, and I consider you wonderful." He kissed her long and hard—a kiss that pressed into her being and left her breathless. The second kiss took her mind away and tugged at her body in a way that she hardly remembered. His arms easily wrapped around her and held her warm and contented.

He drew her to her feet and said, "Dorrie, I am not walking you to the bedroom; I am going to feed you dinner." He kissed her again lightly and led her to the kitchen where the Chinese carryout aroma had already filled the room. "We don't want to waste time but we don't want to miss the journey. When it is time for me to take you to my bed . . . *you* will tell *me*. He ate her Moo Goo Gai Pan and she ate his General Tao's chicken until they were no longer hungry.

After dinner, sitting with music in the background, they let conversation flow and simply enjoyed being together the rest of the evening. He retrieved her overnight bag from her car and showed her the guest room, where Dorrie spent her first night in Jacques' home. "Tomorrow has got to be wonderful, too," she thought as she drifted easily to sleep.

Jacques did not go easily into sleep; the woman he wanted was too close. The day was too perfect, and he knew there were some things he needed to tell her but he could not bring himself to spoil even one minute of this day. He would have to do it before he could take her to his bed. "Why is everything so complicated," he wondered. His days in court taught him it is often what you do not say that causes the most trouble; he should have told her about Suzette.

Dorrie woke early and thought immediately of the man sleeping in the next room. She could not imagine being in bed with him. The older body screams in the mirror and exposure is an old nightmare. How do older women present their body to a man that has not shared that knowledge gradually through the years? Her arms wrinkle sadly when she lifts them, her breasts point down and the skin on the tummy and buttocks looks like left over crepe paper from a long forgotten party. The aged body that presents itself well in nice clothes and proper makeup is a terror when it steps from the shower. In all her concern, she did not wonder what age had done to Jacques' body.

Nor did she imagine that he was worried that his physique would be less desirable to her, and he was not at all concerned about what age had done to the woman he was falling in love with. Neither knew that each was more concerned about themselves than their counterpart.

In the kitchen, he was waiting for her with fresh coffee. What a pleasure it was to have someone to greet at the start of the day, even more pleasurable when it started with a kiss. She cupped her mug of hot coffee between her hands and inhaled the rich aroma with an appreciative smile as they talked of their plans for the day and of the possibility of being together in the evening. Anticipation hung between them like a piñata for a marvelous occasion.

"Will you stay here again tonight?" he asked.

"Is that an invitation?"

'Dorrie, you can consider that room yours, anytime. You can stay here if you need to and if you want to. I have a key for you." He slid a key and a piece of paper across the table to her hand. "That first number is to this answering machine so you can leave me a message. You already have my cell number. I have to hurry off for a 9:30 appointment."

"I am calling Dr. Drysdale to see what time David is coming out of the coma. I am anxious to go home and regroup, but I know I will have to stay a while longer. David will need me."

"Me, too." he said as he tussled her hair and headed for the door. "I hope David is better, but please don't go to Delaware today." There was an element of wistful begging in his voice.

Dicey did not have to be at the hospital until 1:00. That gave her time to get herself together. She needed time to go to Kohl's to pick up some necessities for this extended stay. She needed to call Jen, too.

"Mom, I was waiting for your call. Do you have Allen Herbert's number? He has called three times for you. Says it's important. Can you call him back? I have his number if you don't."

"I've got it. I'll call him before I go to the hospital."

"How are you? Where did you stay last night?"

"Jen, I am fine. I stayed in Jacques Marquette's guest room and he has offered it again if I need it. David is being brought out of the coma at one this afternoon."

"Let us know if you are coming back tonight . . . and Mom, take care of yourself."

Dorrie could not believe the way things had turned around in the last day and a half. She had two strong allies, Jen and Jacques, who were aligned to help, when she had felt so alone the day she packed out of David's apartment. As she dialed Allen's number, she remembered that she had not gotten all the information he had when they had lunched last week. As much as she avoided the boisterous man, today she needed to let him have her ear.

"Hi, Allen. It's Delores. You wanted to talk to me?"

Allen started a-mile-a-minute, as was his manner. She held the phone and let him go.

"Delores, are you in Delaware? All I get is your answering machine so I called Jen. I want to ask if you know a friend of David's named 'Dicey.' I am not sure if it is a man or a woman but Suzette, you remember her, she had lunch with us. Anyway, she seems sure it is a woman. Suzette has called me three or four times this weekend asking if I had talked to you about this Dicey person. Today she called from Malta. She does something for the government. I guess they pay for her calls. Anyway, I hope when she calls again I can tell her I asked you. Do you know anyone named Dicey? Has David ever mentioned anyone by that name to you? I know he never did to me. Suzette thinks this person has stolen David's stashed cash while he is unconscious. Evidently, Suzette checked his safe and it is empty. Now she is hiring someone to find this person. You know with David's business, she can't call the cops. I feel sorry for her, crying over how much she loves David. She thinks he is going to die before she gets home again on Saturday."

It was amazing how this man could say so much without seeming to breathe. While he was talking, Delores prepared the answer to cover all his questions.

"Allen, David is coming out of the coma today. Suzette can ask him about this person herself. Let David tend to his own business as he always has. No one can steal from David King. No one. You know that. And . . . Allen, David is not going to die."

As if he did not hear a word she said, he repeated his question. "So, should I tell Suzette that David never told you about Dicey?"

"Sure Allen, tell her that." It was time to end this call.

CHAPTER 9

There was time; she did not have to rush. Her mind was on trivial things. She would stop at Kohl's, shop for some personal items and maybe some gifts for the girls. She would park a distance from the hospital door and get a brisk walk. Maybe it would be a good idea to get some groceries and cook for Jacques. Her mind was everywhere but focused as she walked to the car and pushed the auto key to unlock the doors. Dorrie hardly noticed the figure that approached the car from the other side, grabbed the passenger's door and entered simultaneously with her. The first reaction was adrenaline that set her irregular heartbeat pounding a non-metered message in her chest as she hesitated in mid-step. "Get in, Dicey," said the accented voice. She was only slightly less scared when she recognized Suzette. Dorrie got into the driver's seat as her knees buckled under her, but did not shut the door.

Suzette was not in Malta; she was here in the street in front of Jacques' house, climbing into Dorrie's car. Experience kept her questions to herself. An old oft-used technique that kept the ball in the court of her adversaries left Suzette responsible to say something to explain what was going on here.

"You are Dicey." she accused; Dorrie said nothing. The whole confrontation was spontaneous when Suzette saw the familiar woman coming out of Jacques's home. She had come to see him when the door opened and Delores Grant emerged. Luke Horton told her that Jacques was meeting David's special person and in a flash, it all came clear to her. This woman was at the hospital that day, she was the one David gave something to at the bedside. Patrick saw her and she fit his description. She has the money David handed her, she has his latest winnings, and she cleaned out his safe . . . and, she was coming out of Jacques's house. Suzette was eaten by jealousy and righteous greed. She would not let this woman take everything, including

Jacques Marquette. "You and David. A good secret, well kept, until now. I know you have emptied his safe. I know everything."

"Actually, you know nothing." Dorrie's composure contrasted the excited, purpose—driven woman.

"Give me David's money."

"No."

"Then you admit you took it. You have no right. Where is it?"

"Suzette . . ." she started, trying to inject calm with a soft appeasing voice. "David will tell you himself . . ."

"David is dying. He can't tell me anything." Her exasperation was building as Dorrie failed to condescend to her. The air was teeming with her desperation, engorged by the unruffled composure of her intended target.

Dorrie did not expect her to pull a gun, even when her hand dug into her purse; she did not foresee a recklessness that would produce a weapon. "Make no mistakes, Dicey or Delores, or whatever you call yourself today, I am not leaving without the money. David was going to take care of me and you showed up, moved in, and took the money. We are going to straighten this out now." The sun flashed on the revolver and punctuated the words Suzette spewed.

Time stood still as the unreal scene, which included a small, retired woman from Delaware and an exotic frantic woman holding a shiny revolver. Dorrie had a flash of feelings that included the willingness to die since widowhood taught her a new lesson on death. She felt calm, resigned and she had a gut feeling that she was in more danger of the gun firing accidentally than by a deliberate act by this distraught woman, but the danger was just as real.

"Suzette, don't do this. I don't have the money."

"You know where it is. Why were you at Jacques? You think you can move in on David and Jacques, too."

Dorrie's mind was too busy to think about those words and what they implied. "Get out of my car," she said as she closed her door and put the key in the ignition. "If I had what you want, I would give it to you. Believe me, I would not risk my life for money."

Suzette glared at Dorrie, stunned by her defiance, and shaken. She could not believe this woman was challenging not only herself but also the gun.

Suzette had believed that when she confronted Dicey she would get what she wanted without using the gun. She brought it as a prop; she did not know if it was loaded and she knew nothing about firing the weapon, which she took from David's nightstand. She had expected to be confronting a woman of little strength from the darker side of David's life, possibly one of the dumb, good-looking ones who hang on his elbow when he is winning. She had not expected to recognize Dicey; she had not expected she was the woman who had had lunch four days ago with Allen. And, she did not expect a woman with a commanding strength.

She was more than surprised; she was undermined. Still, she was committed to challenging Dicey for the money she believed she rightly deserved upon David's death, and if he did not die, she would be the one who saved his money *from* Dicey.

Dorrie retrieved her cell phone from the depths of her purse.

"Don't use that phone." Suzette commanded.

"Nine . . . one . . ." she repeated with each beep. Suzette wanted to grab the phone but she had a heavy gun held by both hands. It was a juggling scene as she tried to steady the gun in one hand and reach for the phone with the other. She began to see herself as a ridiculous woman with a gun she could not use, a demand she could not enforce, a situation that she could not control. She could see no logical conclusion. The scene screamed with frustration. They both knew the confrontation was over.

Suzette bolted from the car, holding the door ajar to cast back her final barb with a wicked laugh.

"I hope you succumbed to Jacques charms and gave him the money; he will give it to me." She recklessly pointed the gun at her own chest with those words, realized what she was doing, dropped the revolver and ran.

Dicey sat in the car, frightened after the fact. She got out, went to the passenger side and gingerly picked up the only gun she had held in her life and placed it on the floor of the back seat. Her heart was beating irregularly. She would have to sit there until her heart and her mind were willing to continue with life. She would not cry; tears seemed too insignificant. Delores Grant was a part of David's life, but it was a game . . . before this week. It was an action movie, a time away from reality . . . until this past hour. Jen's words, *people do crazy things for money* rushed back to her. If David died, she would be in a very risky place. Besides Suzette, who else could come looking for her and all that money which she never wanted to even touch? David was not the only dangerous person in the gambler's world. Two losers who paid up yesterday might feel entitled, too. Finally, Suzette's claim on Jacques brought Dorrie down. She not only knows him; she is confident he will betray David and return his money to her! Dorrie had not only put David's money at risk; she had played a hurtful game with her own feelings. Was she wrong about Jacques Marquette? Doubt swept over her. He was not her rescuer—not her light—or her future.

Dorrie was shattered into tired, age worn pieces that seemed impossible to reassemble. The gun did not discharge a bullet into her body but Suzette's words penetrated her hope of reclaiming a youthful happy place with Jacques. She was devastated; the hole blown in her future was deadly. The unfired gun had ended a dream. "Future," she said with such disgust that it sounded like the filthy four letter F-word.

Dorrie was good at compartmentalizing but it was difficult to concentrate on driving to David's bedside. Suzette's actions and words were thwarting every attempt to sort the important from the ridiculous.

She spoke to the rear view mirror. "Foolish woman! You belong in Delaware."

The only thing she could do as she drove the few miles to the hospital was repeat to herself, "David is not going to die. David is *not* going to die. David is not going to *die*."

The whole medical team, which she recognized from Saturday, was gathered around David's bed. Dr. Drysdale took her arm and walked her to a lounge.

"Ms. Grant, are you alright?" He misread her demeanor. "Do not worry. Mr. King will be fine. We have a little time to talk, as you know this process takes 15 to 20 minutes. The first thing we will be looking for is Mr. King's sight. He should see light immediately; if he doesn't, it is a bad omen. Let us assume he does." He smiled and she grabbed the warm confidence he offered. "Do not worry about his memory, it will be spotty. I mean specifically memory of the last week. He will not have a problem with things he knew before coming here. You will be surprised at how astute he will be immediately."

Dorrie felt better and let the events of the morning fade in to the background. Nothing matter except David's recovery.

"Remember while he was in the induced coma, there was healing. The brain is amazing. The biggest problem will be his strength. We hate to have a post-surgical patient in bed for so many days.

"What about his recovery, doctor?" she asked, a slight catch in her voice.

"He has been getting therapy but that doesn't really hold his strength. Rehabilitation will be required. As soon as his surgeon says, we will move him to the rehab center on the fourth floor. We do not expect any paralysis but he will be disappointed when he moves his limbs. That is really the strength issue."

"He will hate the idea of going to rehab. Selling the idea will be my job?"

"Yes, it will. However, he has no choice. Do your job well," he laughed. "A cooperative patient does much better in rehab."

"Do we expect his son here today?"

"No. He went back to California; he has to work. I am to call him as soon as possible. A very nice and caring son; he was sorry he had to leave. I will be back to get you in a few minutes."

Dorrie sighed in relief. David's son would not be here and she was sure Suzette would not show up here after their encounter.

When David began to come back into the world, she was standing as close as possible to his face. She did not want her voice to tell him she was there. He spoke her name, "Dicey." Did he say it because he saw her or because he was calling for her? It was a horrible moment that brought tears to her eyes.

Please, God, she prayed silently. *Let him see.* She looked into his eyes, which did not seem to be focused. He closed them as a doctor brought a brighter light close. For a small eternity, she held her breath.

"Don't cry, Babe."

He could see! Her tears fell onto his hospital gown.

"I'll cry if I want to, David King."

The doctors moved her away and took charge.

"Don't go far, Dice. Don't let them push you away." He was coming back to his assertive self, but when he raised his arm, it fell like an empty garden hose. The doctor assured him that the important thing was he could raise his arm, strength will come back. "Is Patrick here?"

"You have been out longer than we figured and he had to go home to his job. You will get a call from him this afternoon." David did not ask about Suzette. He complained about blurred vision and was assured that in a few days it would improve. They raised him to a straight-back sitting position and he could see Dicey standing behind his team. A weak crooked smile bent his mouth.

She smiled back and he thought she was the most beautiful thing he had ever seen.

His vitals were taken and a liquid diet was ordered. Dicey stepped forward to do the job the doctor had given her. She wanted to talk, but he wanted to pull her to him, cursing his weak arms. She yielded to him and with her head resting under his chin she spoke to him about rehab.

"David, you will be going to rehab for a few days."

"No way, darlin'. I have been here long enough. Take me home . . . to our apartment."

It took a while, but she convinced him that he had to do this. His effort to move his legs to the side of the bed were useless and he caved to the inevitable. He would be moved to rehab in the morning for possibly four or five days, depending on how hard he worked.

"Dicey, I'll go for two days," he insisted.

If she were a betting woman, she would wager on taking him home in two days. In less than thirty minutes, he was exhausted and drifting back to sleep. The doctor's pleased looks and relaxed attitude told Dicey that it was perfectly normal for him to drift in and out of sleep for the rest of the day.

To keep her mind engaged and away from the events outside Jacques' home, she worked a crossword puzzle until David was ready to talk to her again. How soon would he be ready to hear of the events of the past five days? She had no idea; she would have to follow his lead as he asked to be filled in.

* * *

"Dicey? Dicey!"

"I am right here. What do you need?"

"Don't leave."

"I'm staying right here. You will sleep off and on; I'm working a puzzle and watching you sleep. Very exciting," she joked.

The duty nurse walked in as he asked his next question. She had the answer for him.

"Where is my cell phone?"

"The lady that accompanied your son asked for it. She took it home to recharge it. Here is your bedside phone. Do you need help making a call?"

At that opportune moment, the bed phone rang and she handed it to David.

"Suzette, where are you?" "Malta? How long? Yes, they tell me I am doing fine, but I am very weak. I know; me too. No one. Patrick went home. Why did you take my phone?"

Dicey was wondering what lying reason she gave him as an answer.

"Rehab. Two days, if I have my way."

CHAPTER 10

The late afternoon sun dressed the window of the intensive care room as Dicey returned from a dreary meal in the cafeteria to find David wide-awake and waiting for her.

"Dice. I thought you left and couldn't recall if you told me you were. I'm lost without my cell phone." He looked so much better; color had returned to his face.

She could not resist going to him with a hug. "I was hoping you would feel like talking before I go . . . but if you want to just sit quietly; I can do that." She smiled but he could see it was forced and weak.

"You look tired."

"I'm fine," she lied.

"I do want to talk. There are many things I want to tell you."

"There are many things I want to tell you, too." She reached over to hold his hand, and although she tried, she could not take her feelings back to last week when she walked into this hospital. It was not that she saw him differently, but that she saw herself differently and she could not ignore all that had happened.

Although she had serious doubts about Jacques Marquette, she remembered how strong and motivated she felt with him, and those feelings seemed to be redefining her feelings for David. Jacques Marquette had affected her so profoundly that she was no longer willing to ante into David's world and play the odds that life would be good enough. She was not willing to cast her lot into the world of intrigue, guns, money, and unsavory characters. Was she waiting for David to change? After all these years? And, if he did, would she be willing to elevate their relationship?

At this moment, David had her attention, but he sensed something had happened. Something more than exhausting her, it was changing her. Something in her eyes told him she was pulling away; she was looking at him differently and he supposed that the last days had been too hard on her.

"I am so sorry that I didn't have time to talk to you about the surgery. Did the doctor tell you what's going on?"

"Actually, he didn't have the chance before I figured it out. I do know that Dr. Drysdale is an oncologist and he has admitted that he will continue to be your doctor even though this surgery was not cancer. David, I have been around cancer enough; if the oncologist is still your doctor there are other reasons."

"Yes." David carefully and fully told her about the diagnosis in his lungs. She brought to his news her own experience with lung cancer and knew two sites in the lung precluded surgery, the only real chance for a good outcome. He would be rolling the dice for time with chemo and radiation and he would have to weigh time against quality of life.

Dicey went to him, helped him to move his legs over so she could sit with him on the bed while they digested his news together. They drew mutual comfort from each other as a couple who've been together for many years.

It was a new experience for the usually self-centered man; he was concerned about what his diagnosis meant to her. "You don't know how I hated telling you. I had to have this tumor removed or there would be no quality of life, short or long term. They said I would be blind in a matter of weeks, and I knew, whatever time I had, I wanted sight. The doctors were scanning after finding the tumor when they found the cancer."

"That would be serendipity. You might not have known about the cancer."

"Is that a good thing? I'm not sure. I had some plans, which I would have gone ahead with . . ." He trailed off into thought. "I was about to retire and make some big changes, then I got the diagnosis I had to rethink some plans . . . that included you."

"Me?" She turned to him but he had shut down. She had seen it before when feelings were getting too real. She opened a new deck. "Did you tell Patrick about the cancer?"

"No, not yet. I thought I might die in brain surgery and save the trouble." He made a feeble joke. "The odds are really bad on this, Dicey. There is no good bet on this."

"I know."

"Forget what I almost said. This is no time to . . ." He stopped in midsentence and for the first time in their long history, there were things that needed to be said, and he could not. It was too late. He came very close to making a life with her—marriage—the whole ticket. Now with the cloud of cancer, it was too late to admit how much he loved her. Need had cleared everything away and all he could see was her. He could not propose to her now, after all these years with his future reduced to nothing and his days reminding her of the final ones with her husband. Impossible. If time and love could not bring their lives together before, cancer could not now.

She was confused and could not follow his train of thought; maybe he was still under some anesthesia influence. If there was a point, she did not get it. If he was making any sense, she could not discern it. His cancer changed everything for Dicey, too. No matter how foreign his life was to her, she would be with him. The woman, the gun, the threats, would not be factors in decisions Dicey would make with David. She was not afraid, especially now, with David's presence so strong. She never cared about David's women, but this one had taught Dicey a lesson. A pointed gun is its own teacher. She and the gun made Dicey finally ask herself the question Jen had often asked, "What is wrong with this picture?" She did not belong in David's world. This long awaited knowledge came ten minutes after the realization that the impending triumph of cancer would keep her right here with him. Suzette's presence hung like a black velvet curtain across their stage and Jacques Marquette seemed to step through the curtain as a masked player. She shook her head to clear it of the images that were plaguing her.

"Dicey, you are off in space somewhere." He called her back to him. "Tell me what you are thinking about."

"You know, David, I am very tired. I will come back in the morning and we will talk. I have so much to tell you. It would take all night. You must be tired, too."

"OK. We can do that." Since she did not bring up his business matters, he assumed the collections were made and the money in his safe. She could tell him the details tomorrow. "I'm not tired, but I can see you are worn out." Dicey picked up her purse and prepared to leave the room. She bent to kiss him goodnight when he took hold of her with re-found strength. "Thank you for coming. I really don't know how to show how much I appreciate you. I have always dumped people out of my life, except you, and I know it is because you would not be dumped. I would give you all I have, but you won't take anything. I love you, Dicey . . . . really love you." He kissed her again.

She left with his kiss and he knew she had not given him the echoed reply that had passed between them for decades. Getting out of the hospital room and breathing new air was compelling. She looked back and watched the hospital door close behind her. For a moment, she considered running back to join him on the other side, but instead, she drew a deep breath and continued to walk away.

Dicey called Jen, and got a room at the Hampton Inn. Her overnight bag was still at Jacques's, but it could stay there. With the items she purchased today and a few toiletries which the hotel provided, she would be fine. It was not even six, but she had to admit she was tired and needed to stretch out and rest. She hated going to the hotel room where there would be nothing to distract and keep her from revisiting her time with Jacques and Suzette's final words. There were calls from Jacques filling her voice mailbox and torturing her. She checked in and turned off the cell phone for a while, although she knew she would have to turn it on again. Jacques was not the only one who could possibly call her number tonight. Dicey had a good hour and half nap before the room phone awakened her. She picked up the receiver with trepidation but heard a welcomed voice. "Dice, how are you, Babe? Did I give you time enough to rest?"

"Yes."

"I tried your cell, voice mail and, the apartment—no answer and no answering machine, either. I knew you'd be at the Hampton. Why aren't you at the apartment?

"It's a long story and one of the things I will tell you about. How are you this evening?"

"I'm moved to room 411 in rehab and feeling pretty good. Ate dinner. Since you are so close, why don't you sneak in to see me? I kinda hate to close my eyes again."

Rules at the rehabilitation floor were more relaxed than on the other floors so she was able to get in before visiting hours were over and stayed past them without notice.

"David let's think about the immediate," She said shortly after arriving. "If, and I say *if*, you get to leave rehab in two days; you will need help."

"I thought about that when you went to eat. The nurses got me up and it took two of them to help me walk four or five steps. I want to work hard to get my legs back, and I admit it will take time. I am really weak. Look, I can already lift a drink with my arms; even put them around you. That is an improvement since I awoke this afternoon. I would like for you to go with me to the apartment until Suzette gets home. I don't think I told you about Suzette, did I?" There she was—Suzette. Her name was in the air. Now that he mentioned her, Dicey had no choice. She had to talk to him about the woman. How could she even begin to tell him about her meeting with Suzette without going through all the things that happened while he was unconscious? Was it too much too soon after his surgery? She pulled a chair close.

"David, there are some things I must tell you and I need to be looking at you when I do."

"Babe, there is something wrong. I knew it. Don't tell me those collections went bad. I never should have asked you to do them."

"Actually, they were the easiest part of the week. Your money is safe. It's Suzette."

"Oh, Damn!"

"She is not in Malta; she is here. I saw her this morning. She was determined to find Dicey and she did. She demanded your money. Of course, I didn't give it to her. She was at the apartment, too.'

"You mean our apartment in Takoma Park?"

"Yes. I just want you to know that if you talk to her again. She's lying."

She did not tell the details of her encounter with Suzette, but, she recounted her story about the apartment and the safe, she watched clouds of anger pass over his face. If he were not compromised by his illness, there was no doubt he would have been flying into action.

"David. I am not going to tell you all of this if you cannot control your anger. It is not good for you to get excited. I took all the things in the safe, including the collections and the envelope of papers. If she got in the safe as she told Allen she did; she got nothing. I have it all."
Dicey did not tell him where the items were. She did not know if she

could trust Jacques but she did have the deposit information for the escrow account.

"You know my temper, Dice."

"For me, please, darling, don't let it go." She got up and went to him, placing her hand on his chest as if to calm and appease him. "The important thing is that you know you cannot trust Suzette, and that I have your assets safe. What else matters?"

"It matters that *you* are safe. Tell me about the meeting with the bitch."

He was getting angry thinking about Suzette's audacity and Dicey was not going to feed his anger with the details. He was not going to know about the gun.

"I basically ignored her demands and that made her angrier, and then I just drove away."

"I am so sorry that you had to deal with her and her foolishness. She is really harmless and I know why she acted as she did. You see, Dice, we were finished. I think the inevitable was delayed by my illness. She's afraid I was going to split and leave her with nothing as her last long relationship did. I'll bet she didn't expect me to survive this," he said pointing to his head. "And, she doesn't even know about the cancer. Suzette is very accomplished, but insecure. I am not making excuses; just stating facts. When our relationship ends, she will be homeless and I promised to make sure she had the means to get her own place. She may have been more worried that I would die than anyone. Foolish broad. I always keep my promises."

"David, I will tell you all about my meeting with Suzette, but not tonight. It was upsetting, but in the whole scheme of things, not important." If he knew about the gun, there would be no holding him in this bed. His body would respond in such a way that the rehab staff would be amazed. His temper was legendary and she knew him well enough to fear what he would do to himself. Dicey also knew she had to go easy in telling him about trusting Jacques Marquette, especially since she did not have the confidence she had hours ago when her feeling for the man fortified her decisions. "I was going ahead to pay your hospital bill and unload a lot of the money as you told Dr. Drysdale I would. But, think of it—how could I walk in here with thousands of dollars in cash?" He had to laugh at this, and it was good that they could share a light moment before she got into deep water with him.

"That is funny, Dice. I never thought of it, being a cash-and-carry man all my life. Of course, I didn't think you would need to find a place for the money. I figured you would have only to pay the bill if I died. I have accounts, but you don't know where they are. You could have looked into my papers to find my accounts. I am sure you did not do that."

"No, I didn't."

"I didn't do a good job, taking care of things. I thought three days; you at the apartment, me in a coma, the money in the safe and I'd be back in business . . . . didn't work out like that, did it?"

Hardly."

"You should not be carrying all that cash around with you. Where is it?" His concern, she could see, was her, not the money. It was time to tell him about Jacques and the escrow account. She was afraid she might show her feelings when she had not sorted them herself.

"Jacques Marquette," there, she said his name, "set up an escrow account and we deposited it in the bank."

"Marquette?"

"Yes. I went to him for help. He charged you a retainer to do this and to keep your papers in his safe. I had to trust someone. We made it a business deal not a personal favor. We couldn't put that sum of money in an account in my name."

David noticed her repeated use of the pronoun *we.* "You are right; you couldn't. Escrow is good. You went to Marquette? Did you know him before you made my collection?"

"No . . . . but he gave me his card that day and I took a chance. He couldn't have been more helpful. Since he knew you and understood the monies, I didn't have to do any explaining except that you were in a coma. I felt very threatened, especially after Allen told me that Suzette had hired someone to find me. Jacques's solution seemed like a perfect one to me. I hope we did the right thing."

David's demeanor changed as she sat looking directly at him. She could see him shutting down with a cold grey steely gaze. There was no way to read what he was thinking. Was he angry that she had trusted Marquette? Did she make a mistake? Surely he could not know what was churning in her heart. Even as tears filled her eyes, he was unmoved by her obvious distress.

"Maybe today has been too much for you. I know it has for me. I think I will go home in the morning and regroup." It was the lowest point she had felt since this all began. She took his hand. "It is only a hundred miles; I'll be back. Get that cell phone so you can let me know when you need me."

It was the lowest point for him, too. Something in the way she talked about Jacques Marquette stayed with him. Cancer seemed minor to the sense of loss he was feeling for Dicey. Nothing could account for his conviction that he was not going to be able to finish his love for her. He would not make up for lost time; he had no time. Cancer would make sure of that. There would be no winning, no big payoff; he was a loser just like all the losers he had known. When this debt was paid there would be no next time to make up his losses.

"Dice, you did the right thing with the money. Your instincts are always good. Go home for a while. I am going to be fine. Come close and tell me good night."

"Good night, David. I love you." She kissed him in the traditional manner and gave him a smile that recalled many secrets between them. He held her an extra moment as she gave into it as if all the years between them could be wrapped into one embrace which along with her smile would get him through the night and take away his fear of closing his eyes again.

"I love you, too."

Either he had lost his number one position with her or she was already preparing to face his death. If it weren't for the cancer, he could conquer any competition, master any problem, and overcome all odds to have her and hold her. David was tough and he had done some tough things in his life. This would be the hardest. He had no choice; he had to let her go—not just to Delaware—he had to set her free. They both knew the truth: he would be the one leaving; she would never go.

*   *   *

Life's choices were easily made by David. He was philosophical about it; you win some, you lose some. He believed it and he lived it. Not only did he believe in his right to make choices, he accepted the right of others to make their own choices. Just as he accepted other's choices he expected others to accept his. And so, he lived his life without blame and without accountability—his own version of the Golden Rule. It was a good working philosophy. He only ran into trouble with it with Dicey. She was not a live-and-let-live person. She had all these principles and morals that were plain nuisances. As long as he could remember, he wanted to be with her, and when he was, he could see they were too different to stay together. It was better to find a woman with fewer levels, less depth, and therefore less important. The result was he went from woman to woman and she learned to be thankful he had never asked her to marry. It would have been disastrous.

He was tempted to try to keep Dicey for himself when he got out of jail, and planned to propose. He was full of redemption and good intentions; she was full of stories of a man she was about to marry. Dice looked good; aglow with love and he had never seen her so enticing. Her sexuality could not be denied. David even told her, "Greg is a lucky man and I am forever a fool. Why are you marrying someone else?"

She took his remark in good humor and shook her finger in his face, "Maybe, because you never asked me." Both knew that was not the reason. Each time he resolved to do so, he hesitated, knowing he could never take her into his dangerous life, knowing, too, that she would hesitate and create a memory that would be forever awkward. "I have already told Greg that I have loved you since second grade. You can't guess what he said."

"Tell me."

"What gambler would hedge his bet so long? He deserves to lose."

"I like that man; when do I get to meet him?"

In truth the two men met and did like each other, but David could not bring himself to attend their wedding. As happy as he was for Dicey, his own emotion was too real to deal with. He sent a large check which was never cashed.

The second time he was tempted to claim her was after she spent six weeks with him while he recovered from heart surgery. The problem this time was she was still in love with Greg even though he had been dead almost two years. David's faith in choices had become a religion, almost Presbyterian in doctrine. He was here; she was there and that was that.

Although she prayed for him constantly; David never thought to go to God in supplication until he got the cancer diagnosis.

"Please God; I don't want to be a burden to Dicey. Throw me the checkered flag. Give me the final buzzer. I'd rather die today"

He knew he would call her; he knew she would come.

CHAPTER 11

Dorrie should answer Jacques's calls; she was just postponing the inevitable. Deep down she knew he would not stop calling until she did. The phone rang while she was driving to the motel. This time, she had an excuse for not answering—she did not talk on the phone while driving, but she promised herself to take the next call. The message was the same, "Please call me." She was dressed for bed and ready to turn off the television when she admitted to herself that she was disappointed; he did not call again. That put the ball in her court and she did not like it. It was much easier to decide to refuse his calls than to make the decision not to call him. It would be a long night since she had napped earlier; she was not sleepy. David was strong on her mind; Jacques was strong on her spirit. A strange thought entered her mind. If all was good with Jacques, it would be easier to see David through his final months.

She could not keep her mind from the terrible events of the day. The words that Suzette threw at her this morning were not to be ignored. The woman was confident that Jacques would betray her. It was obvious she had been going to his house. She had a relationship with him. The thought was far more distressing than Dorrie thought it should be.

Why hadn't Jacques mentioned knowing Suzette? That he hadn't was more conclusive than the angry woman's words. Jacques was hiding something from her, and it was possible that David would be betrayed in some way. She and Jacques had only been together for one day, one night, two kisses. That wasn't much. It was time to forget about him and move on. "It is time to get back to my real life and stop acting like a teenager," she said aloud. The generic decorations in the poorly attempted colonial style of the motel room seemed the perfect backdrop for the woman who could not clear her head, could not sleep, and could not see beyond this night.

As the first light came in the window, Dicey finally drifted off to sleep. She dreamed of leaving and driving, but every time she got out of the car, she was still at the hospital. Her mind kept telling her she knew the way home, yet each attempt brought her back to the same place. Finally Jacques walked up to the car window . . . . and rang a bell. The vision of him brought her out of the dream and to the reality that the motel phone was ringing.

"Hello?"

It was David. "Dicey, I thought you would be gone. I tried your cell and then this."

"What time is it?"

"9:45. Are you OK?"

"Yes. I didn't sleep well until early this morning. I've got to get going."

"I am starting therapy at ten. Just wanted to tell you to take care. Drive carefully."

"I will call you when I get home, OK?"

"Suzette called this morning, said she got back from Malta early. She is bringing my cell phone. We shall see what she has to say."

"David, don't lose your temper with her. Whatever you do, don't set yourself back. It isn't worth it."

"What I really called to say . . ." His voice drifted off.

"David? Are you having trouble telling me something? It's me, Dicey. Tell me."

"Dice . . . I won't need you. You've done enough for me. I can manage. Suzette will stay with me if I offer to pay her."

"If you work it out with Suzette; it is none of my business, but that will have nothing to do with me and what I do for you or with you. You know that. It seems to me that you are worrying about things that are not the prime concern right now. Get your strength back; make decisions with Dr. Drysdale. Then we will talk about what you need and who will help you."

"Babe, you are always right."

"I know." They laughed together and he almost forgot about Marquette and so did she. He had not accomplished what he tried to do with this phone call.

At the same time that Suzette walked into Richard's room at the hospital, Jacques waited outside of Dorrie's home in Delaware. While he waited for her to drive ninety miles, he was going over in his mind the words he would say to plead his case. Ironically, his emotions prevented the lawyer from organizing his thoughts in a professional manner. *Suzette is nothing, nothing . . .* he thought. *You are everything, everything . . .* he almost cried. Jacques wished, waited, and worried.

Meanwhile, back in Maryland, Suzette walked into the hospital wondering how she would be received by David. Jacques and Suzette, who were once a couple, now separated by the Chesapeake Bay, ventured into unknown territory wondering how they will be received by Dorrie and David. They have more in common today than they ever did. Each must explain themselves well or risk losing much. The difference is Suzette wanted David to give her the means to go on alone and Jacques wanted Dorrie to give him the chance to never be alone.

Dicey's trip through Annapolis was smooth. It was a good thing since her mind was not on the drive. The only bright spot was crossing her beloved Chesapeake Bay where the beauty never failed to touch her. She took a deep breath and lowered her speed to 55 and let all those who exceeded the limit pass. Getting to the other side seemed to have some hidden agenda for her. Which side of the largest inland bay in the United States, western shore or eastern shore, held her life? She managed the rest of the drive, without getting into serious thoughts about her future geography. She began to look forward to the comfort of her own home. She turned into the development and waved to a few neighbors and reminded herself that she had only been away one week; it seemed a lifetime. She pressed the garage opener and did not notice the car parked just beyond her mailbox until she turned into the driveway. It was Jacques.

He watched her drive into the garage. He could not walk to the door where common courtesy would bring an invitation to enter. Jacques didn't want politeness. Emotions raged as the minutes ticked by. He reached for the door handle twice and withdrew. *I can't make her . . .* he thought. "Why did I even come here?" he said aloud as he looked once again at the secured entry. *Please open the door, Dorrie.* His thoughts pleaded but brought no action from the quiet house. It was a long ten minutes before his cell rang.

"Jacques . . . . come in."

The door opened as he reached for the knocker and he came into her world where all was bright and beautiful. Coffee was brewing, cups were set, and the screened porch beckoned.

As they entered the sunny room and took seats across from one another, she was aware of the joy she felt seeing him, yet did all she could to deny it.

She looked wonderful to him, but very tired, and the light in her eyes was gone. There was not one spark of happiness to see him. Maybe he should just turn and leave, but he was at the rail, and the lawyer in him would say what he had prepared in his mind for the last thirty-six hours.

"Dorrie," he addressed the judge. "I am sorry that my first time here is not welcomed, but your leaving was more than I could stand. I have not betrayed your trust in me. Do I deserve the right to explain?"

He was a good lawyer; his words were persuasive. She knew he deserved a hearing; he had done a good turn for her and for David. She nodded assent, not trusting her voice to betray her feelings.

"I am sorry Suzette accosted you outside my apartment."

He spoke in a steady stream; she was the most important jury he had approached. "Suzette and I were in a relationship before she met David. I was in love with her, it is true, but she wanted more than I could afford to give her. When she went with him, I was heartbroken, but I assure you, that was over a long time ago and I am not in a relationship with her now. I do not have any feelings for her. Suzette is all about money, and when I realized that, I considered myself fortunate to be rid of her. After my law practice grew and I prospered, she was interested in me again. In fact, about two months ago, she propositioned me. I think things with David must not be good. I hope you believe me. When you came to me for help with David s's money, I didn't see any need to say I knew Suzette. Then, when we had such a special time together, I realized that I needed to tell you, but I never had the chance. Yesterday was the first time I had seen her in a long time. She came demanding I tell her where David's money was. I don't know how she knew I had handled it. I did not tell her." He paused and repeated. "I have not betrayed your trust." He was hardly breathing when he added, "Please believe me."

It was a long speech and she listened to every word intently. She wanted to hear things to make everything right. It was a matter of trust and faith and it was overwhelming. Sitting there was impossible, so she stood and ran out of the room, but before she passed the doorway, she turned to the man and raised one finger as if to say, *give me a minute.* In that gesture, Jacques took hope and waited.

She did not deserve this set of circumstances, but life was not about getting what one deserves. Dorrie's mind was reeling with truths about David and Jacques; she was tortured by loyalty, torn by love, battered by compassion, and, utterly shattered by passion. She knew herself. She had spent a lifetime giving up her inner-most being and ignoring her own desires. Today she would act accordingly. A minute or two to compose herself and she could go back to the porch where the man, who may or may not understand her need to finish her life with David, waited.

She returned with the coffee pot and warmed their cups—a symbolic warming. She was tending to him as she had always done for the men in her life. His gaze was locked on her, but she did not return his gaze until she sat across from him and tasted the coffee.

"Jacques, I have never propositioned a man in my life. We have three and one-half days before I have to go back to Maryland. Could we spend them here, together . . . before I return? That is all I have right now."

The world seemed to pause on its axis. Jacques knew it meant she would return to David on Monday. She was making a choice. He knew it and she knew it. Devotion to David would take her away again but he wanted what she offered. David was not the only gambler in this game. At any table, at any race, at any time, anyone can win. *I'm in,* he thought, full of confidence.

"Dorrie—" he rose to go to her "—as I said before, let's not waste a minute. Shall we go to the beach? I have a place in Bethany. Come with me to the beach." His arms wrapped around her and gave a warm, strong feeling she had missed immensely for the last few days. "Pack." The kiss he gave her was fully shared and deeply felt.

A phone call interrupted. He listened to her side of the conversation and filled in what he imagined were David's words.

"I'm fine; how are you? . . . Good. I'm glad you are staying until Monday . . . Of course. It is so good to hear you sounding so much stronger . . . I know; there is a lot I need to tell you when I get there. David, I am going to Bethany with a friend . . . . I do need some time, you are right about that. The beach always does it for me. I'll leave from there Monday morning. Call me on my cell. You don't have to do that; call me anytime . . . I love you, too."

Jacques could hear the gentle feelings she had for the man on the other end, but he did not hear any passion or longing. He would use his time to show her what she was missing.

*   *   *

Jacques' place at the beach was just north of Bethany in Blue Heron Dunes. It was an imposing house with private beach access. Dorrie noticed the wide balcony facing the ocean and could hardly wait to park her tired body and soul there. She had always found solace in the action of the waves and the magnitude of the sand, sky, and water. It was as if she could sift, wash, and spread out her conflicts in this space that speaks of God. If it worked for her this weekend, it would be a miracle.

Her things were dropped in the foyer and she went for the sliding door to the balcony; he let her be with her thoughts while he put her bags in the master bedroom facing the same scene. His personal items and some clothing were moved to the guest room; there would be no assumptions. The beauty of senior love is priorities and knowing the wants and needs of the flesh are important, but they will not melt away or lose wonder by waiting for the right time. Jacques and Dorrie were aware of wants, needs, and timing. With a tray of ice tea, he finally went into her space where she was waiting for him.

"Jacques, this is a beautiful place. There is nowhere on earth I would rather be than here with you. I cannot tell you how special I feel." The feelings she savored were strange and long buried ones that, before today, she never wanted to recall. She was heady with the excitement that now, after being so long alone, she would find someone to chase the hours with joy, maybe even fun. There was brightness in her inner being that was overtaking a gloom that she had become complacent about and hardly knew how much it darkened her. Something here with Jacques erased the years, the tears, and the fears, like a miracle. When age has begun to define life, even three and one-half days can seem a gift beyond measure. Jacques was the brass ring and she wanted it while they were on the merry-go-round.

"You are special to me. We need to understand what this time together means. I can be your friend; I can be your pastime, or I can be your lover. I want to be all three. Does it make you uncomfortable to get this straight, up front?"

"No, as a matter of fact, it is good. I want you to be all those things, but it is only fair for you to know that we will have only this time. No more." Dorrie hated to say it again, but she had to be honest. "I am going to be with David on Monday." Was she saying this? How could a woman of her integrity and basis accept all that Jacques was offering her and in the same breath admit she was going to another man? She hardly knew herself. "He almost proposed to me yesterday and I believe as he recovers, he will again and I will accept."

It was tragic news but he kept his composure. "Is he doing well; will he recover? Did you say brain tumor?"

"Yes, it was benign."

"Well, I hope he does fully recover but I can't help, but hope he won't propose again. He never has before, has he?"

She smiled, "No, never . . . but if he doesn't propose, I will. You must understand; I am going to be with David. Do you still want this weekend with me? It is selfish and unfair to you, but I . . . more than anything . . . I want this time. I want to be with you." She rose to go to him and he drew her to himself. The only six words that meant anything to the man were: 'I want to be with you'. He was going to take a chance and stand pat on the hand she dealt. Jacques Marquette was not a foolish gambler. The odds had to be good, and he believed that possession was 9/10 of the law.

"We will not waste time. Get changed for a walk on the beach to build a good appetite. I know a great restaurant that is a half-mile up the beach. You will love it." Dorrie rose to do as he said and promised herself to let him decide everything that happened in the next three days. She was tired of making decisions. She was tired of weighing consequences. She was tired of taking care of others. She was tired of being in control. She was tired of her life . . . .

What a surprising thought. Was she really tired of her life? At her age, could there be new life? One thing she knew, as a senior, the chance to find out would, most certainly, never come again.

*   *   *

Suzette visibly shook as she entered the hospital and inquired for David's room. Her courage was gone, as was her conviction that she was justified in her actions of the last few days. Moreover, she did not know how much he knew. The quandary was whether she should confess everything or wait to see what he knows. As she walked down the corridors among the sick, she had her first qualms about his health. What was she going to see? Maybe he will be so sick, so weak that her confession or supplication will not be needed. She could have saved herself that thought. David was sitting up, reading the sports page from the Washington Post, and looking strong except for the exposed stitches across the left half of his skull.

She stood in the doorway, waiting for him to feel her presence. When he looked up, she said, "Ami", in a very soft voice.

"Suzette. I've been waiting to see you." There was no smile. She stepped in, but instead of approaching him, she took a chair from the corner as a child who is prepared for a scolding.

"Dicey has told me twice to hold my temper with you," he said in his usual direct manner. If I manage to do that, it will be because of her. Suzette, you made a big mistake. You know that?"

"Oui."

"Quit that French shit!"

"I will move out, but I need some time: I have no place to go."

"Suzette, you won't be moving yet. Make no mistake, we are finished, but I am going to give you the chance to redeem yourself and pay me back for your stupidity. You went to my apartment in Takoma Park?"

She nodded.

"Did you mess it up?"

She nodded.

"You will go back there and set everything straight. If there was any damage; fix it and pay for it, too."

Suzette was gaining her composure, especially since David was not locking her out of Watergate. She did not know where Marquette was and he did not seem willing to take her back. Horton was a squirrelly type and she would never turn to him. Her options were limited at the moment and she was grateful that she could go back to Watergate. David's tasks were not that difficult; she could have his Takoma Park apartment ready *in a few hours. It wasn't that bad; she had taken some anger out on the surfaces, thrown things around.*

"David, your safe is destroyed. I'll pay to replace it, but I don't know if I can do it by Monday."

"Forget about the safe. Just get the apartment ready. Here is a list of items to put in the kitchen. Do that Sunday evening so they are fresh. Got it?"

"Are you going there when you leave here?" *She knew he would not be going there alone.*

"Yes."

"How long do I have to get out of Watergate?"

"I'm not sure. You know better than to take anything from there that is not yours, don't you? Play your cards wisely, Suzette." *He warned. An uneasy silence fell between these former lovers as she stood to leave.*

"I'm glad you are recovering," *she said from the door.*

"And . . . Suzette. Stay away from Dicey. Understand? Go about your life; live at Watergate; go to work . . . . and answer the phone if I call. Don't call me unless it is an emergency"

She turned and walked back to the bedside. "David, I am sorry; this is not the way our time together should end. Is there any possibility we could go back and start again?" *She knew she had no place to turn and she needed this man and his support. Begging was not beyond her pale to get back to that place of comfort she had with the gambler.*

"Not a chance; the game is over. But I am not turning you out on the street; I have always told you I would not do that . . . . didn't I?"

All in all, this had gone better than she expected. There was no doubt, Dicey did not tell David about the gun or she would have been exiled or worse. I wonder why she did not tell, *she thought. She still had a roof over her head, and a fine one at that. It would have been nice and easy if she still had David, but since she was not emotionally tied to him, she felt no great loss.*

David knew she would stay at Watergate as long as possible, even while trolling for a new benefactor. She would surely stay long enough for him to finish his life. He did not cast her out; he held on to Suzette because he would need her before it was all over.

CHAPTER 12

Dorrie studied Jacques. He was what he seemed to be, honest and forthright. She did not have to be anything false with him. He accepted her life with Greg and the crazy part that was David, with assurance that they were part of her past and he was her future. It sounded wonderful, but she knew otherwise. There was no more room in her life.

She was a bit troubled; he seemed to ignore the fact that they only had these few days. Dorrie never for a moment forgot and went at each minute as a child savors and quickly eats an ice cream cone before it melts, knowing, by eating or melting, it will all be gone—one way or another.

Everything was perfect, the beach walk, the dinner, the stroll back to the house. It was pitch dark with ocean sounds and a million stars. Dorrie and Jacques did not talk as they walked hand in hand, and when they ran from a rogue wave he held tight to her as he tripped and took her down with him in the soft dry sand. "Let's stay here for a while, unless you are chilled."

"I'm not cold" She could not be warmer and she recalled her promise to herself to let him make all decisions this weekend, large and small. He held her close as she began to talk of the things she had missed for so long; the touch of a loving man, the strength of hands that could keep her from falling, the person who could tell her what to do and have it be exactly what she wanted to do. A man who genuinely cared that it was something she wanted to do. A woman never forgets the wonder that come with happiness; she is always aware that wonder, like the stars at night, will be diluted by either time or light or most probably both. Jacques saw that she was giving him every sign and clue to keep her in his arms and to lead her to his bed. It was a heady thought. Is it possible that her barriers were coming down? Her abandon in giving him this weekend could mean the moon and the stars to him. "Tell me what you are thinking?" she asked.

Men are not easily led into personal confessions, but he wanted to stay on equal ground with her as she opened up to him. "Dorrie, the things, that I feel, are coming from you. Some I had never thought of until I began spending time with you. You are special, a gentle spirit and a beautiful woman; I have found a comfortable place with you that I did not even know I was looking for. I do not believe I will ever know enough about you, but all that I am learning and feeling is filling a deep, dark, empty space in me. I believe I could spend the rest of my life exploring what you are."

She lost her breath when he talked of the future but his mention of a deep, dark space struck a common thread with her. Her life had been circling a deep dark space since Greg died. She had planted her life, her activities and her aspirations around it like a circle. Jen and the girls were on the circle; David was on the circle and her retirement community was like a flowerbed around the dark precipice. The things on the rim grew and grew with time but the circle never closed; the deepness and the darkness never shrank. The widow had stopped trying to fill it; she accepted it and only looked into it during her darkest hours. Jacques was not speaking from the rim of her circle. He was reaching across it.

They slipped off their shoes to let the sand caress their feet. When coolness began to come, he dug the sand to reach the heat stored during the day and covered her feet and legs with the strangely warm sand he brought up for her. It was a small, silly thing that children on beaches have done for years, but it seemed to have great meaning for Dorrie, almost animal and erotic, as he took an element of nature and passed it to her, tending her body and allowing them to stay a while longer in this place. She ran her hand across his chin, turning his face to hers; she took her finger and traced across his moustache before he kissed her outstretched finger and she kissed his lips. It was a different kiss, staying on her lips and mind. He could not see the two tears that slid down her face as she pressed her head to his chest and began a new kind of good bye to Greg.

"Let's go home." He drew her to her feet. Inside, he turned on the fireplace to take the chill of the night air away as they went in their respective rooms to shower. They met back in the great room by the fire, dressed in pajamas and robes, neither wanting to end the evening. She saw the firelight dance highlights on his blond hair and he noticed the wet curls clinging around her face. They both felt young and beautiful—and the power that comes from those feelings. "Shall we read together? I have a book of American classic poems." They took turns picking and reading favorites while a bottle of red wine helped the fire to warm their world. She drifted off as he was reading from Longfellow's Day is Done:

> "Then read from the treasured volume
>   The poem of thy choice,
> And lend to the rhyme of the poet
>   The beauty of thy voice."

Jacques let her lie there in the nook of his arm as he listened to her quiet breathing and smelled the vanilla scent of her. His desire was such that he had to let her sleep; it was his only control but as his voice went to silence, she missed it and roused from her slumber. "Jacques."

"Yes? You dozed off. Henry Wadsworth put you to sleep."

"It is the wonder of the whole day that put me to sleep . . . and the wine."

"I didn't want to wake you and have you leave me to go to bed. It's better to stay here. I should've kept reading." He moved a stray curl from her cheek to behind her ear, using his fingers to find her neck. Dorrie leaned into his touch; it was not the burning touch of young love, but the comforting touch that was full of commitment and desire.

"I should go to bed; I'm thoroughly exhausted. Can you come with me until I am asleep? Jacques I cannot have you completely." He knew what she meant. "I have just begun to say good bye to Greg. Do you understand? Am I asking too much? I need you close to me while I bid this farewell. We could stay here on the sofa . . . ."

"We will go." He rose and took her hand to walk her to the bed. "Dorrie, go to bed and sleep. I will come to be beside you as soon as I secure the house and fireplace." He kissed her lightly, tucked the comforter around her, dimmed the light and left the room. Jacques took his time with the tasks so he could think. It had been a long time since he had shown such restraint. This was love and he spoke the word aloud—*Love*—not sure if he was getting his mind around the emotion or giving the woman with so many names, a new one. He was dwelling on her announcement that she was finally saying good-bye to Greg. She had never done that to be with David. His hopes soared that maybe, just maybe, when she had reconciled her devotion to Greg's memory, she would know that what she had here with him was worthy of surrendering that devotion.

Sometime in the night she knew he was there making the cocoon that made her metamorphosis possible. It was a cocoon of robes, comforter, arms and legs holding her safely until she could emerge and be the new person she wanted to be. Sleep came back to her and she took it like a gift. Meanwhile, he was awake most of the night, turning in response to her, holding and letting go as her night dance required. Jacques was much too aware of her and his desire, to sleep. A smile crossed his face as he accepted that it certainly was his age that made such patience possible. He was much too wise, and too much a gentleman, to act on his beating heart and hungering body. He wanted more than this night. He had dreams. The soft light finally announced the impending sunrise and she roused.

"The sun is coming up," she announced to herself. Dorrie never missed the sunrise when she was at the beach. She stretched and pressed against him feeling a great contentment. "Jacques," she said softly looking into his eyes, "let's get up to see the sunrise?"

"Dorrie, we don't have to. I promise you will see it from right here. Look over there, through the third row of windows. The sun will soon be in your eyes." He raised his arm to point and lowered it across her bosom where she intertwined her arms to keep his weight on her breasts. She pushed closer to him and he could only wish that her pajamas, a sheet, a comforter, his blanket, his robe and his pajamas were not between them. "There, look, the horizon is broken. A new day." She kissed the shoulder that was handy.

"I have to get up, Dorrie. I cannot stay here; I want to make love to you, too much."

"Show me Jacques. Show me how to get out of this cocoon," she said as she began removing the layers between them. It was the beginning of a day of discovery as two lovers took themselves to old heights and new thrills. The senior bodies were not old, they were not ugly, nor were they uninviting. They were right for each other, right for the moment . . . Right forever.

And, *right* is all any lover can hope for. He was strong; she was wild. The pent up fire broke through her as a flame blows open a window for the air it needed to burn. Jacques was amazed but not nearly as amazed as Dorrie. There was something in the culmination of intercourse that was pure animal and left the lovers satiated yet not complete. If they shared love along with their bodies, they would always hunger for each other again to reach completion, and with love, the act would always be prelude to the next. In the early morning sun, Jacques's and Dorrie's lovemaking caused an appetite, not just for more sex, but for completeness.

Jacques finally slept as she rose from the bed, made coffee, showered and dressed for the day. In the quiet time alone she reminded herself that this was a time away from reality. Jacques would be disappointed—more than disappointed, devastated—to know that her decision to go to David was unchanged except for one thing. She would not marry him. She would leave Jacques and her heart here on the beach and go to David for as long as he needed her. The only way to do that was to break off with Jacques on Monday, but she could not, in the glow of their lovemaking, imagine how she would do that. There was no other way. She would go to David totally, wholly, and without stringing Jacques along. Dorrie was a woman of principles; her principles were gutting and butchering her.

She put these thoughts out of her mind and went to the sleeping man with a tray of fruit and coffee so they would have some sustenance to continue doing whatever he decided for the rest of this day, the next and the last.

* * *

Many times she had tried to explain David to Jen. Dorrie's daughter struggled to understand what brought her mother from the good life in Delaware to this man. Jen really liked David, everyone did, even her father, who seemed to have no problem understanding their bond. Jen did not approve of David's lifestyle—gambling for a living. She even ignored his prison record, but the thing she held against David was his inexplicable hold on her mother, especially in the years since her father died.

One cold winter day, Dorrie traveled to Jen's specifically to explain David. Jen had to understand, if possible. It would not be easy because the woman herself had never been able to understand why this man was such a big part of her life. Hopefully the words would come.

"Jen, I love David and he loves me." These words crushed the younger woman and she began to fight the tears welling in her eyes. "Don't cry; please don't cry." The last thing Dorrie wanted was to hurt her daughter. "I don't love him as I loved your father. I will never go to his bed." Jen was confused, but her mind opened again, after shutting down on the opening remark. "Let me try to explain. There are some kinds of love bonds that fall somewhere between family and sexual. David and I are there—but I cannot define it. I am the only person on this earth who sees him as he really is. His life is false; except me. There is no reality in the chance a card will fall right. There is no truth on the probability of a win, no goodness in the neon and flashy people he deals with. He cannot make a living any other way and when he left jail he was a changed man. Changed on the inside. The dichotomy is that he continues his lifestyle, and with me, he can have his own inward truth. He has studied the great philosophers of the world, but he is not strong enough to live what he believes. That is another contradiction in his life. Look at him. He is so big and strong but there is no inner strength. David will always accomplish the things that can be done with brute strength, beyond that he needs me. He knows his weakness and believes it is because his mother died when he was six and I have some long-standing connection to his mother. As a mother sees the good in her son, I see it in David. He loves me, very much. Too much to try to keep me in his world. I started loving him when we were in the second grade. He was my first crush, my first love, my teenage infatuation, and my idol, like Elvis, but I never thought he was my life. David was my scrapbook-life. You know my love and devotion to your father; surely I don't have to prove that to you again."

"No, Mom. I know that." Jen smiled for her mother and it was the greatest gift she could receive.

Dorrie continued, "Now that we are older, David's physical strength began to wane and his need for me grew, coincidentally with the loss of your father. As he needs me more, I find I need something from David. I want to be with a man . . . . and I am not talking about sex. Jen, *you know I miss having someone other than the ladies to talk to. I hate getting my dinner tab, pumping gas and doing the million things a man does for a woman. I hate dressing to be seen only by women. There are so many things I miss that may be silly, but they are profound now that I am alone. When I go to David, I am not lonely and that is the bottom line. He is there when I open the door; he is there when I come out of the bathroom; he is there to turn on the news in the morning, he is there to disagree with me, he is there to laugh with me . . . . and he doesn't make any demands on me. He just wants me there and he wants to tell me how important I am. Once I told him, I would not come to his bed,. Jen I am being honest with you . . . he never asked me again." Jen stepped to her mother and took her in her arms. "Jen, if you understand, it doesn't matter if anyone else in the world understands."*

That last statement was true when Delores Grant said it, but that was before Jacques Marquette.

CHAPTER 13

Delores and Jacques made the most of every minute. He unplugged all the clocks, put their watches in the drawer and punched in 0:00 on every electronic eye in the house. The only time they observed was sunrise and sunset. They played each other like fine musical instruments and laughed at their mutual exhaustion. She cooked for him; he cooked for her. They walked the beach and picked up shells. On Sunday night, wrapped in each other's legs in front of the fireplace, they had chocolate for dinner. She let him talk of the future, but he noted she said nothing to confirm or deny there was one for them. If she had, she would have to *go there* and she refused to look beyond this day.

"The National Symphony is doing its Brahms concert on the 28th." It was just a fact; she did not acknowledge that it was a search for a plan. Even without clocks, both were aware that the time was ticking away. He had to say it before they slept. Try as they would, they could not stay awake after a day of lovemaking. "Don't leave me, Dorrie. I am begging you. Marry me, or not—just stay with me. Let me love you forever." She was so still he could not feel her breathing although she was as close as she could be without being inside his skin. Jacques took her shoulders and turned her to look in her eyes. "I'm not the only one falling in love here. I know it."

It was impossible to answer him. She nodded but said nothing. She could hardly breathe, let alone, speak. She could only draw him back into their embrace and think about every place where his body joined hers; head to chin, breast to breast, hip to hip, loin to loin, arm to spine, ankle to ankle. She breathed in the smell of him and took a taste of his mouth. She needed to remember everything. When she was sure he was asleep, she whispered in his ear, "I love you." He slept content that she could never leave him. When he woke for the sunrise, she was gone.

As the sun broke the horizon, Dorrie was traveling west with tears staining her face and wetting her blouse. If she had stayed for the sunrise, she would not have been able to go. She promised herself that she would never rise early to watch the sunrise again—ever.

Her note was short:

> Dearest Jacques,
>
> Leaving you is the hardest thing I have ever done. I will hold fast to the love you have shown me and the love I feel for you. It is more than I ever hoped for. Nothing has changed. The reasons I go to David are the same. We love each other, too . . . . but not in the complete way you and I love. I cannot explain.
>
> When I asked for this weekend with you, I had no idea that three days could mean so much. If I had, I would not have put us through this parting.
>
> > Love,
> > Dorrie

Jacques sat with the note for long time. When he moved it was to get out of this house where his dreams had been fulfilled and dashed. He headed west too, but he was not trying to catch her. She was gone, and he was simply following the double yellow lines back to an empty world.

Dorrie pulled into an empty parking lot and dialed her phone. "David, good morning. How are you?" she started her conversation to tell him she would be there soon. He was excited to hear her voice and knew that she was coming to him.

"I am discharged and can leave whenever you get here. Our apartment is ready for us. I even had some food brought in. How are you, Dice? Did you enjoy the beach over the weekend?"

"Yes. "There was a pause, ever so slight, but he noted it. "See you in about an hour. I'm stopping for coffee at McDonalds before crossing the bay bridge."

"Drive carefully. I don't want anything to happen to you."

She turned off the phone and gently banged her head against her hands clutching the steering wheel. "Something has already happened to me," she said to the rearview mirror as she checked traffic and pulled onto the highway.

David held his dark phone and waited for an uneasy feeling to pass. *Something is wrong,* he could tell.

He was dressed, sitting in the chair watching Fox news when she came into the room. Dicey was beautiful, tanned, and smiling. Seeing him looking so well lifted her spirits. Her smile was real. Her greeting was genuine, but her kiss was light, swift, and perfunctory. She recalled her feelings for him, but wished it had not been only three hours since she had been with Jacques. It was hard to change feelings. "What do we have to do before we leave?"

"Ring for the nurse and we're gone." He stood to hold her. "I am glad you're here." His earlier doubt was relieved by the sight of her.

"Me, too. I couldn't be any other place."

David waited until they were settled in the apartment to talk to her. He let her bustle around putting away their few things and making ice tea. She seemed to need some time to settle down with him.

"Dicey, I have some things to tell you. First, I know you are willing to stay here and care for me, but I am not going to let you do that. I'm going to let Suzette do it. She owes me for her actions." He was always about settling obligations. This announcement was a total surprise to her and her face revealed it. She kneeled on the cushion beside him, facing him as he continued.

"Babe, I'm not opening a discussion," he said firmly, stopping whatever she was going to say. "I'm telling you what I'm going to do."

"I have something to say . . . ." She tried to speak but his hand gently covered her mouth.

"Oh, damn. I hope you are not going to throw in some common sense, are you?" He smiled the smile that had won her over and over for many years as he put his arms around her.

"David I knew when I saw you Thursday morning, you were about to propose. It took me a while to figure out what you didn't say. Now you want to send me away. Tell me I'm wrong."

He would not lie to her, so he did not answer her question. "I've had time to think. I spent the whole weekend deciding what I want to do. My mind is made up. There is something else . . ."

He was a stubborn man, and she had never been able to change his mind before. This would probably not be an exception. She turned on her haunches and snuggled to him. "David, hold me close while you tell me what else you have decided."

For the first time since she walked into his hospital room he felt he had his Dicey back. "Dice, I am *not* going to have treatment. I have read everything I could get my hands on. I understand small cell and non-small cell cancer, and I have both. I also understand stage four. To gain two, maybe three months, I would have to have treatments three weeks on and two week off until the cancer gets me. I would rather have one good month than six bad ones. Look at me; I am *not taking the treatments.*"

"Fine, I can accept that, I will stay with you and we will spend whatever time you have together. Do you think I would be content to be in Delaware now? Please send Suzette away." She pleaded. "I deserve to be with you. I want to take care of you. Look at me—" she took his face in her hands "—how can you send me away?" She dropped her hands, released his face, crossed her arms on her chest and said, "I won't go. You and Suzette will have to deal with it."

His baritone laugh at the feisty woman filled the room as he pulled Dicey back to his chest. It was familiar territory that had often welcomed her. As she settled there, he became serious again. "Now hear me out. Suzette and I are finished as a couple. I told you that before, but we are taking a quick trip to her native Haiti as soon as the doctors let me go. There are reasons . . . something I must do. You can trust me on this, can't you?"

"I have always trusted you, David. You know that." She had a history with him that included mystery and unfilled gaps. His motives and actions were never questioned for details and this undisclosed, unexplained trip was part of his life's pattern. Dicey let it go.

"I understand your feelings toward Suzette—rightfully, too—but I must finish this thing with her. After the trip, she will go her way, and I will go mine. You can be the boss of whatever is left of me." He drew her closer with all his strength. "I want *you* to take care of me—I just hate to put that on you, but I am not surprised at your insistence. In fact, I love you for it, and will love you for eternity. No one else can fill whatever time I have . . . or my heart . . . only you."

Dicey got up from the sofa feeling like she had stepped off the world's longest roller coaster. She was a little dizzy and needed to take air standing alone. The early morning with Jacques seemed light years away. These tender moments with David were wrought with bittersweet memories. It was too much.

David took her hand and pulled her back down. "Dicey . . ." She yielded herself to him. She gave her strength, spirit, and total support to the man who was of her past and who was planning his final days. She was who she was. There was no changing now to a selfish woman who longed to be someone else, somewhere else. "Agreed, I will be with you until the doctor says you can travel, and I will be here when you return."

"Thank you for refusing to leave me. I really don't want Suzette here, but I need her for this trip. You see, Dicey, I want to be with you until I leave. These next weeks are important to me. I want to tell you all the things I never said. I want to soak up being with you and try to get past the regrets I have."

She smiled and patted his check with her forefinger. "Not you, David King! . . . Regrets? I've **never** heard you mention regrets."

He took hold of the finger that was chastising him and continued seriously. "I regret that I didn't love you enough to keep you with me. I regret that I didn't change my life enough for that to happen. I want to make up for it. Stay with me."

It sounded so much like the plea that Jacques had made in the wee hours of this day that she was in physical pain from the words. She gave in to tears. There was only one way to be with David without continually weeping—she had to put Jacques totally out of her mind. She'd been right to leave him; there was no way she could see him while being true to David during his final days. Her love for David, which was always laced with memories, was now laced with pity. "I will be here with you.'

"It is not much of a life, is it?'

"It is my life. My life is here with you, David. How soon will the doctor release you to travel?"

"At least two weeks, maybe three. Suzette has to schedule time off, too."

"And how long will you be in Haiti?"

"Maybe three days."

"I will be here when it is over." David was struck by her choice of words and lowered his head into her hair.

They spent the evening curled together on the sofa talking of old days and old friends. The high school yearbook and picture albums were spread on the coffee table. They almost forgot about the cancer, except for the cough that had invaded his space and seemed constant.

"Will you come to my bed, Dicey? I will be honest with you, my illness and my medications . . . . I am impotent. I just want you there." He misread the tears in her eyes. She nodded, "Yes." It was good that he thought she was disappointed that they would not have intercourse. They would finish their lives together without physical consummation. She was saved from an awful guilt that could have destroyed her.

"I did want to propose; had decided to ask you . . . . then I got the cancer news, he said before giving in to sleep. It is my loss that we never married. You're right, I almost proposed on Thursday."

"I almost said, 'yes.'" This was the hand they were dealt; this was the hand they would play. He had what he wanted. She had perimeters she could live in.

Jacques was part of everything that was said here today. I have not really left him at all she thought,

*   *   *

Death is a special clarifier. It takes shades from eyes, revealing goodness taken for granted. It takes fog from distant planes so the horizon is claimed. And, it takes magic away from the future, giving today the importance it should have. Death is everyone's companion and yet, it is stowed as if it belongs to someone else. David faced death several times in his life and always thought his would be played out on the stage of his lifestyle—swiftly, and most likely—violently. Cancer changed his final act as he had authored it and gave him this terrible alternative.

While Dicey was at the beach he used the days to work things out in his mind. Suzette had been banned from visiting, Patrick was in California, and Dicey was gone until Monday. He had the time. One major decision was quickly made. He would refuse chemotherapy; his time was counted in weeks and he intended to feel as good as possible in the time he had. He would not squander that time, hoping for more to be sick. It was decided. Dr. Drysdale had already been told.

Dicey was harder to think about. How could he send her away? All these years she had refused all his gifts, and he wanted, more than he wanted his next breath, to give her the gift of freedom—freedom from him and the problems cancer presented. He could not seem to find a way to make her leave him. Now as the clock ticked away the weekend, he knew she was getting her life arranged to come back to him. Nothing was more frustrating than trying to find a way to keep her out of this mess.

The irony was that with the clarity he had recently acquired, he was consumed with Dicey. His desire to have her was as strong as his surety that she must be sent away. She was his first thought in the morning, his lingering longing during the day, and his tearful regret before he slept. The memories that he treasured were those crazy days during which they carefully moved around their care for each other. The gambler had never, in his whole life, wanted something so badly, and he had never had so much difficulty making a choice or accepting the only choice he had. How stupid. How foolish. How selfish he had been. Now, he had to do the ultimate unselfish thing for her. As sleep came gently to him, he thought of her saying Jacques Marquette—*the way she said it. The look on her face told him what he didn't want to know . . . .*

That knowledge inspired in him a determination he shouldn't feel—a need to hold her as long as possible.

CHAPTER 14

There were things that had to be taken care of before David and Dicey could settle into their new routine. Dicey needed to drive to Frederick, see Jen, and explain what she was doing. David needed to get things in order for his trip to Haiti.

Her job was easier. Jen accepted her mother's decision to be with David for the rest of his days. She did not tell her about the weekend with Jacques. Jen would have a different opinion about the events at the Takoma Park apartment, if she knew that.

While Dicey was gone, David called Suzette to tell her to prepare for a trip to Haiti. "Haiti?" she asked incongruously. David knew she never wanted to go back there. Bitter haunting memories engulfed her at the mention of her native island. "Why do you want to go to Haiti, and why do I have to go with you? Are you asking me to be with you again?"

"Hell, no! That's over."

Suzette responded with a casual shrug of her shoulders, which he could not see on the other end of the line.

"I have some final business to take care of there and I need you to go with me."

"No, David. I have not been to Haiti since I left as a *fille* and I don't want to go back now. You know that. Don't ask me to go." she pleaded.

"Your mother is still alive there, isn't she?"

"*Oui*, as far as I know." She could not help the bits of French that crept into her language when talking of her mother. "*Mon mer*—my mother—is still there." Talk of her mother made it harder for Suzette to accept the idea of going back. She had spent twenty years erasing all memory of her mother. She did not want to think about her and she certainly did not want to travel to the red dirt and green jungle of Haiti to see her. *Porquoi mon mere?* She wondered.

"I want you to take me to her."

"Why? I don't understand . . ."

You don't have to understand. I am going to make your future secure if you do as I ask. The Watergate condo will be yours. Frankly Suzette, here's your choice, if you want the condo, you will do this."

"If I go to Haiti with you . . ." she was considering the price and the reward. ". . . for how long?"

"Three days."

"You are going to give me the condo, free and clear?" She was calculating the value and slowly dismissing her feelings about returning to Haiti and seeing her mother again.

"If you do as I ask; you will have earned it."

Suzette wanted the condo and the financial independence it would provide. She would not have to look for or depend on another man. She stopped concerning herself with questions about why David wanted to go to Haiti. All she could fixate on was the condo, a small thing for such a big reward. Of course, she would do it, just as David knew she would. She should have paid attention to the last words he spoke. David was always true to his word.

The days went by quickly. David and Dicey enjoyed being together, each knowing it was for a short time, and making the most of it. It was like playing house—Dicey cooked and cleaned while David took care of business on the phone. Keeping busy was her salvation. She did not want to have time to think about David's death. Shortly after he returned from Haiti, with complete surety, she knew the rage of cancer would consume their time and space. There were times when she wondered if she would be able to face it again, but tried not to go forward in her thinking. She did not want to go backward to Greg's final days either. Both directions were overwhelming for her.

She filled his Percocet prescription and knew he was taking it regularly for pain. Soon that medication would not be enough. Hospice was not mentioned but she promised herself that when he returned, she would present the idea to him. He would need them and so would she. Fussing and pampering gave her great pleasure and filled her mind during the day but on the second night, she crawled from bed, went to the dark living room and thought about Jacques. The sun dancing on the ocean, the warm sand at night, and the peace she found in his arms were wonderful memories, but they were pushed aside by guilt which washed over her in the dark. Although she knew things always looked worse at night, she knew she had done a terrible thing to him. No matter how the game played out with David, the only chance she had for real happiness was gone. The cry, that she could not scream, dried in her throat and brought up her dinner.

The domestic scene suited David—maybe it was his age, or his illness, or his delight to be with Dicey. Most likely it was all three. Not since high school, had meals for him been placed on the table regularly. Dicey prepared old fashioned family meals of pot roast and fried chicken. The man who knew every restaurant in Washington and suburban Maryland loved the real mashed potatoes, bread pudding and apple pie. He could not resist bringing the cook to his lap to thank her. She was happy doing these simple things for the man of the streets, as she watched a gradual decline in his stamina, breathing and appetite. He made no apologies for his cough; she accepted it, but the sound caused a pain in her stomach.

When he went to the bedroom with his phone in hand; she knew he would be doing business so she took a walk or went to the grocery store. When she returned he was usually dozing in the chair, so she sat quietly waiting for him. "David, are you making book? Will I have to make collections again?" She asked in her most direct manner.

"No, Babe. I am letting all my clients know I am retired. There are a couple of outstanding accounts but 'frankly, my dear, I don't give a damn.'" He smiled and she thought he would rival Clark Gable as the dashing Rhett Butler, not only in looks, but in actions. "I really am retired. I've been working on my portfolio with my broker and taking care of details with my accountant."

"I'm glad I don't have to put on the red shoes again. I'll pack them up for Goodwill. Hungry?"

"Not really, but I know you want me to eat . . . . so feed me." Dicey went to the kitchen to fix sandwiches and he told her what he needed to say while she was not looking at him. He did not want to see her face when he said, "I called Jacques Marquette . . ." She laid the bread out. ". . . about the papers he's holding for me . . ." She placed the meat and cheese on the bread. ". . . and the escrow account." He paused. She put lettuce and tomato on the meat. "I guess you won't be surprised to know after the hospital was paid, very little was left of that money that caused you so much trouble." Still, no sound emitted from the kitchen as she spread mayo on the tomato. "Dicey, would you go to pick up the papers from his office . . . or maybe . . . drive me over there." The sandwich was cut, put on a plate and brought to him.

David took a deep breath and hoped she would not opt to go to Marquette alone. He would have allowed her but he prayed she would not.

"I will drive you after you finish your lunch." She could do that, but she could not chew or swallow her sandwich as muscles tied knots in her stomach. Her emotions were tested while his name was spoken by David here in the kitchen. She could not see Jacques. Not alone. Not today, nor tomorrow.

When they arrived at the office of Horton, Horton, and Marquette, Dicey was amazed at the agility David showed as he left the car and walked to the door. Little did she know that he had called every ounce of his strength and resolve to walk in to see Marquette with all the virility he could muster. With a ball cap to hide his half bald head and the tan he had acquired on the balcony, he looked healthy. In a short time, he emerged, with his papers and a look of triumph on his face. He leaned over and surprised Dicey with a kiss, so unexpected and unusual for them in such a situation. Just as David supposed, Jacques was looking out the window.

"What was that all about?"

"Dice, a gambler needs to win, especially needs to take in the last pot."

She wanted to ask about Jacques; she wanted to know everything that was said in that meeting, but she would never know.

Exhaustion was on David's face as he moved from the car to the apartment. His step and demeanor was a shadow of his effort when he was going in to meet Jacques. Dicey settled him into the recliner and warmed him with an afghan and a hug.

"Dave, have you told Patrick about the cancer?"

"Yes, we have been discussing it and my trip. I asked him to come see me before I go. It might be the weekend before I leave. Will you be comfortable if he is in the guest room? He wants to meet you and I want you to meet him."

"I want to meet him, but I won't stay here while he is here. I will go to Delaware. You need some time with him alone, without me. Let's think about this. If he comes the last weekend and you're leaving Tuesday. I don't want to drive to Delaware on Saturday, come back on Sunday and go back to Delaware on Tuesday when you leave. That is just too much driving. If Patrick stays until Monday, I'll just go to Delaware on Saturday when Patrick gets here and stay until you get back from Haiti."

Nothing prepared her for the look of panic on his face which suddenly turned to anger as his temper flared. "God damn it. Give me that phone. Pat is not coming that weekend. If he doesn't come this weekend then he needn't bother. I wasn't thinking. Those are our last days and I won't have you in Delaware." His face was red, his breathing was labored and a coughing fit scared Dicey. She did not understand his anger but saw what it did to his capacity to breathe.

"David, David! Wait darling, we can work this out. Don't get so upset." She ran to him and brought the chair to the upright position, hoping to assist his breathing and stop the coughing spasm. The oxygen line was quickly placed in his nostrils as he looked thankfully in her eyes. "As soon as you settle down, we will call Patrick and see if he can come this weekend. If it matters to you so much that I be here the last weekend, nothing will cause me to leave. I will be here. Pat and I both will be here that weekend."

It took a few minutes for him to breathe normally and regain his composure. He looked at her with the long familiar steely gaze that she knew was not directed to her but rather the silent rage of a caged animal. She knew she had to leave the room until he had his emotions under control. He was feeling something way beyond her comprehension. In the bedroom, Dicey fell across the bed, prayed for strength, and got up to straighten her hair and emotions.

"Dicey, come here," he finally called. "I wasn't thinking clearly; do you think the cancer has gone to my brain?" He reached out for her hands and noticed how cold they were as he rubbed them with his.

"No. I don't. It's true, lung cancer does go to the brain, but there are usually motor skill problems before cognizance problems. You do not have any of those symptoms. David, you are trying to take care of everything. You are sick, you tire easily, and that explains a lot. Can you be more careful about getting upset? It is too hard on you."

113

"Hard on you, too. Forgive me for losing my temper, Babe." Apologies were rare, and so out of character for him. "I want to see Pat, and as we discussed it, I realize that I don't want him here on the weekend before I leave. There are special things I want to do with you, we are going to be selfish and spend the time alone; no Patrick; no Jen. Just you and me. I am going to call him and see if he wants to meet me in Haiti. Is that a good idea? I'll buy his ticket."

She agreed with him wholeheartedly; it was an excellent idea. Dicey had never wanted to voice her concern about Suzette caring for the sick man even for three days; Pat going was a perfect solution. "I should have thought of that before. I will call him tonight."

"If Patrick meets you in Haiti, do you still need Suzette with you?"

"Yes." He answered, strongly demanding with his tone, that Dicey leave that alone.

The tickets were purchased. Suzette and David would fly to Haiti on Tuesday, July 17, out of Washington National, flight 547. Pat had a ticket to fly to Haiti on Wednesday, July 18th leaving Sacramento on flight 1609. Suzette's return flight had an open date. Patrick's return flight would leave Haiti on Thursday July 19 and would bring him to Washington National. Everything was well planned. David was pleased that Patrick would come to Haiti. His presence will be comforting and no doubt, helpful. He looked at Dicey and thought, *I'm sorry my darling but I know you will understand . . . I must go and do this.*

That night David was pain free and confident that he had arranged everything to the last detail. He was content. Dicey's hand was firmly contained and her body curved to his. He was sure she was content, too. David did not move a muscle, not even to squeeze her fingers. He took time to store in his revelry the smell of her body lotion and shampoo. He noted how her head fit under his chin and the way her heel pressed his ankle. A perfect spell encased them and he feared breaking it. Sleep was coming unbidden as he whispered, "Babe, we should have been like this forever."

She answered his musing with her own sleepy, contented voice. "We would have, if we could have. The important thing is we have what we want now. Nothing else matters. I love you"

"I love you, too, Dice."

*   *   *

Jacques Marquette had no success putting his life back together. He did not have anyone to care for or to fill his days as Dorrie did. His were empty, completely empty. Work and golf were mere distractions to him. He threw himself into a case that required hours of research and documentation—two jobs he usually assigned to associates, but now, to fill his hours, he took on himself. His partners wondered what was wrong with the man. The weather was perfect at the beach in mid-July, but he was seriously contemplating selling the place instead of enjoying the season. Many times he came close to calling her. Many times he was tempted to put a message on her answering machine in Delaware. He never did. Seeing her, or talking to her would not make a difference. It was clear; she had made her decision. There was nothing he could do. For all he knew, she and David could be married by now.

"Mr. Marquette, David King on line 1." Why did he feel excitement to get this call from the man who was most probably standing close to Dorrie?

"Hey, Dave. How are you doing? Are you recovering well?'

"Yes, thank you. I am beginning to get out a bit, and I would like to pick up the papers you are holding in your safe . . . and I need to properly thank you for your help while I was in the hospital." The two men met and the congeniality that they had shared carried them through the meeting, where each had his own agenda concerning the woman they both loved. Marquette asked about Dicey, and that seemed natural enough. David told him she was waiting for him in the car. "I am retiring, Jacques. No more bets. No more clients, no more wins, and no more losses."

"I am sorry to hear that . . . congratulations."

"I think I am a lucky son of a bitch to get out of this business alive and with a few good investments, solvent. The rest of my life will be better than I could imagine." Jacques pang of jealousy was almost crippling. "Sometimes the biggest wins are the ones you wait for until the pot is big and the game is almost over. Can I ask one more favor?"

"Sure, name it."

"The last draw on the escrow account will clear the bank on the 19th. Would you call Dicey on the 20th and arrange for her to get the balance. Call her until you get her that day; I'm not sure where she will be. Do

you have her cell number?" They shook on it, making it a promise. At the door, David turned to make sure Marquette understood. "Call Dicey on the 20th, don't forget. I have your marker on it."

"I won't forget."

David left feeling very smug with his arrangements, his planning and his scheme. Jacques went to the window in time to see him give her a kiss before they drove off.

CHAPTER 15

As Flight 547 lifted from the runway, David took a deep breath and embraced the certainty that he was a dead man. It was strangely alright. He wanted to take a deep breath, but there were no deep breaths left in him. It was time.

The plane cleared the overcast and pushed into the sun. When the seatbelt light went off, he told Suzette to put down her magazine. It was time to take care of business. Get it over with, so he could rest, and think about the last hours he had with Dicey before this mission took him away. Suzette needed to know why they were going to Haiti, and what she had to do to earn the condo. He had everything planned very carefully, yet he had not thought ahead as to how he would tell her. This was the time he had selected, as soon as they were above the clouds and the seat belt light was out, but where were the words? Directness was his only tool and he used it.

"Suz," he used her pet name, which she had not heard for months, "you are taking me to your mother so she can assist me with suicide." He took a breath and let the words slide into Suzette. "I remember the stories you told me of her drugs, and of the old people that she had helped die. Cancer is eating my lungs away and I want to die now. I am not going back home again." It was hard for him to say these words, put them out in the air between them. "Your mother can help me, and you are going to use your state department connections to get me cremated and my ashes ready for Patrick to take home. He'll meet me in Haiti tomorrow. We have 24 hours." He was talking quietly and with great strength. She was staring wide-eyed and straight-ahead, saying nothing.

She turned to look at him, saw his pain and his dire condition for the first time. The face that had charmed her was tattered and worn. Pain deepened his brow and glazed his eyes.

As compassion crossed her face, he read her feeling, raised his hand in a halting gesture and spoke before she could. Though he appreciated the sentiment, he did not want any compassion, not hers, not anyone's. "Suzette, you are here to convince your mother to help me. Consider this a business trip. If it is successful we will both have what we want." It was a lot to ask, but he was confident she would do it.

Suzette raised both hands as a shield against his words, and pushed them against the air repeatedly so he would not utter another word. *God, this is unthinkable. I can't do this.* She understood now—David's insistence on this trip, on seeing her mother. It made horrible sense. And it brought regrets she did not want. Regrets she thought she could never feel . . . was incapable of feeling. *How did I get here?* She asked herself as she lifted her gaze away from David, and searched the plane's ceiling and window for a place that was not a trap.

He saw her eyes and head searching back and forth, and ignored her anxiety. "Did you look at your ticket? The return is open-dated. You can go back as soon as we get the job done or stay as long as you want."

"I'm not going to do this." She still did not look at him. Her voice lowered to a whisper. "When we get to Port-au-Prince, I am staying in the airport to get a flight home. "No." she spoke softly, begging him to let her out of the cage.

"Yes," he contradicted, knowing he'd shocked her, and perhaps hurt her. David took her wrist and held it with old strength. "What are you going home to? Think of what I am offering . . ." He released her and rubbed the redness on her arm as he took a kinder tack. "Suzette, neither of us has a choice. We will leave this game even up. Give me the only thing I have ever asked you for." It was true—he had never asked for anything in their long relationship. He had given and given to her.

"Take me to your mother. That is all."

She did not say a word but slowly nodded her head up and down. *If only he would take my hand,* she silently begged. David would not touch her again, ever. Her wish for something soft, warm and comforting would be unfulfilled. Ice cold blood cursed her veins and brain. She began to shiver. David called the attendant to bring her a blanket. That was all she got from him.

David waited until food and drink were served and the tension had mellowed so he could outline the plan for the next three days. "We will go directly to your village when we land. The urn for my ashes is in my suitcase. As soon as Patrick has them, you are free of all obligations to me. My will gives you ownership at Watergate and spells out what to do with my belongings. It will be changed, if I go home alive . . . well, we won't let that happen, will we?"

David did not notice that she was crying; silent tears were streaming on to her white blouse. There was nothing she could say. It was too late to tell him how sorry she was . . . . for her actions, for his illness, for this tragic ending to their shared life, and for her blindness most of all.

It was too late to thank him for always being good to her, for loving her, and for taking care of her. It would sound like gratitude for the home he was giving her, and it would have sounded so *purchased*—exactly as she was feeling at this moment.

A taxi was easily secured with the generous cash David flashed. She knew that he had exactly the persuader that poor villages along their route would notice. Maybe he had enough money to get what he wanted from her mother. Old memories came back of the cash the man gave her mother, so he could take Suzette away from Haiti when she was a young girl. The money her mother took for her was surely gone now. Most likely she would be happy to take another bankroll for the basics of life, food, and drugs.

They traveled inland over 100 miles before a clearing led to the village of Suzette's buried memories. Poverty and filth were everywhere. The red/brown dirt of the roads and yards was back-grounded by lush green jungle. Between the hovels and the trees, everything was lifeless gray sparked by brightly dyed clothing and t-shirts advertising colleges and rock stars from a far away world. Homes, more like huts, lined the jungle edge. As they traveled, she covered her coiffed hair with a scarf and removed her shoes to slip on plastic sandals that she usually wore in the shower. Her mood was dark and she hardly said a word in the three hours it took to reach their destination. David was pale with pain.

It had been a grueling journey and the hot, humid air was thinner at this altitude. Only one thing kept him going—the reason he was doing it. His gaze was fixed; his mind was set. The worse he felt, the more certain he was that this was the only way.

There was no wavering as Suzette turned to him with a begging, questioning look. She did not want to do this thing, and she did not want to see her mother. David was unmoved by her mood or her begging look. "Go find her. I will wait in the taxi."

David needed to rest and maybe sleep. The driver went to get him some fruit from a marketplace. For this kindness, he was given more than he would make in a year. David ate the fruit and fell into slumber where Dicey came to him in vivid dreams, smiling and happy, but he could not touch her. When he stretched his arms to her, she was always just out of reach.

Suzette returned and looked at David, shocked at the sight of him. Tears threatened again, but she blinked them back. She knew they would not be appreciated. Suddenly, he had become a weak old man. He had aged much since they began this journey.

"David, I have found my mother. I told her who you are and why you need her help. She will not do it." Even as she told him, she knew he would not accept this answer.

David did not notice how shaken she was; he did not care. "Take me to her."

Paschette, Suzette's mother, looked as if she had always been old, but in truth, she, David and Dicey were the same age. There was nothing about the hag that would hint that she had mothered a beauty like Suzette. She was worn, dark, dry leather stretched over thin bones. Her elbows and knees were blackened with age; her eyes were two black holes. When she spoke, large white teeth seemed to pop out of the face in an idiotic smile. It was not a smile. When her mouth opened, the skin on her face had no elasticity, and it fell away from her skull. She was repulsive in every way except for her soft, pleasing voice. David closed his eyes after her first words, and felt the only remembrance he had of his own mother—a soft pleasant tone of voice.

"*Entre vous . . .* if you must."

He raised his hand to stop everyone from going forward with the visit and stepped backward. He needed a moment; he needed Dicey. She would understand what the sound he just heard meant to him. The old woman, misunderstanding his actions, urged him on. "You can come in." It was his mother's voice telling him he was doing the right thing.

Paschette lived in one of the better homes in the village. It was worn and dirty, yet substantial, more than one room. No doubt, she bought it with the money she got for selling her daughter. In a strange mixture of French, native dialect, and English, she told David to go away and take Suzette, too. Suzette stood very close to him and translated the unfamiliar words as if they were meaningless to her; as if she were unaware of being discarded again by her mother. "You waste my time. I will not give you the gift of death. It is *precieux* and can only be given to those deserving. Take Suzette. A*ller!*" she insisted, as she spit on her hand and pointed to the door.

David opened his bag and produced a wad of money. "I will pay well. It is the last money you will ever get for Suzette, but I will not pay and take her away unless you give me the drugs I need." He offered a deal to the woman for her daughter, knowing she had done it before.

Paschette dropped in a nearby chair, dropped her long black arms between her legs, and doubled over until her head rested on her knees. Her struggle with herself did not last long. After a short pause, she sat up straight and spoke to David in pure clear English. "Why should I give you the peace and release you desire? Who are you to ask this of me . . . and why do you have control over Suzette? Is she your puppet?"

Her clear strong questions surprised David and gave Suzette the motivation to speak. What right did she have to question the actions of the daughter she had thrown away? She petitioned her mother, "*Mon mere*, please do as he asks. We do not have a lot of time and must get back to Port-au-Prince. Can't you see David is sick and in pain. He is a good man and faces a long, hard death. You have done nothing for me since before I was twelve. Now I am asking you for something. The money he offers will last the rest of your life." She took one step toward Paschette. "Give him the potion. Do this for me." The words were spoken with passion, as she looked directly at her mother.

The black leathery face did not reveal the woman, but emotion came to her eyes, as she glared at her daughter first with disdain, jealousy, and then a spark of tenderness. Her thoughts went back to that black day when she bid Suzette good-bye. *La fille* must know it was hard to send her away to a better life. Hadn't she been right to do it? *Why didn't he take me instead of the girl? I wanted to go, but he wanted the young one.* Her final thought before deciding to give the gift of death was a wish that there was something more meaningful to give the lost daughter, but this was all she asked—all she would ever ask. The old woman poked her finger in Suzette's chest twice and said, "You will have to wash your hands, Pilot. His death is yours," and stepped back from Suzette and nodded assent to David.

"I tell how it goes. *Le potion* will take your life away in twelve hours. There will be no traces. No antidote. No turning back. *Ce vous prepare?*"

"Yes" There was no doubt, no wavering in his conviction and she could see the relief in his eyes as he realized she was going to give it to him. Paschette took them to a dark room and offered David a cot. Suzette took a chair in the corner still rubbing the place where Paschette's fingerprint burned.

Paschette could see that he was weakening in the heat and humidity; his coughing had worn him out. She would do this thing for her daughter and this man, who were obviously not lovers. She spent no time trying to figure their relationship; it was unimportant to her. Perhaps to pay Suzette for bringing him here, he would set her up for life with his money, too. They could both benefit and be comfortable for the rest of their lives. She left to go for the precious commodity.

David slept. Waiting was hard for Suzette. So many memories pressed in on her in this place. She was most peaceful thinking about David and a new understanding came to her. He was not an ordinary man who had lived within normal boundaries. She began to be thankful that she had a part in giving him what he wanted most at the end of his life. She was wise in the way of lovers and knew he must love the woman Dicey very much. No doubt, he was doing this for her. *He was willing to let me watch him die, but he loved the other woman too much to let her watch.* Suzette concluded that David did not know that much about love, or he would not have left Dicey for this.

"Drink twelve hours before you are ready to die. I give you a good death. You will be very comfortable while you are conscious and will sleep the last six hours. Make your arrangements well." The vial was in David's hand; the money was circled by dark stiff fingers. The deal was done.

As the taxi turned to go down the mountain, Suzette did not look back at the woman standing in the doorway.

The Grand Hotel in Port-au-Prince had two elegant rooms ready for David and Suzette.

No fond farewells were expressed. She did not know what to say as he stepped on the elevator.

"Thank you, Suzette. Good bye and good luck." She watched the doors close, but he never turned and looked back at her.

David went straight to bed and slept out of pure exhaustion, thinking he felt so bad that he might die of natural causes before either drinking the potion or Patrick arrived. This sleep was without dreams, though his last thought was to remember Dicey crying for his mother in the second grade.

Suzette needed to spend time in the bar; she needed a drink. The warm whiskey went down roughly, uncut by a mixer. Memories of happy times with David came roughly, too. There were some good years—most of the years with him were better than any others she could recall. She could move in the bar environment with ease, yet wished David were with her, to order her drink, to keep the barflies away, and to generally make everything nicer. One drink led to another, but she refused the drink ordered for her by the man at the end of the bar. The second drink brought thoughts of her mother to push David aside. Two whiskeys gave her the guts to leave the bar, walk to the entrance and ask the doorman to hail a taxi. Three hours later, with one stop to buy some rum, she again approached the door of her mother's tattered home. She paid the taxi to wait and entered the dark house without knocking or announcing her presence. The old woman was cooking salt fish patties and boiled dumplings, unaware of the intruder. She turned with a start and flung the wooden spoon with expletives that hurt more than the missile. Suzette picked up the spoon and gave it back to her mother.

"I thought you would come back. You want your part of the money. Yaghhh!"

Suzette was not sure why she was here. "I don't want any money. I'm hungry." The old woman did not answer, but brought two bowls to the table with the aromatic, native food, which Suzette thought she had forgotten. There was nothing the two women could say to each other, no common ground.

Except for the pain of birth and rending of the womb, the old woman could not remember her daughter. It had been easier to use the ever-present drugs to erase any thought of the daughter that was dead to her. They ate in silence by the light of a candle as darkness crept in from the jungle. The dancing light enhanced the younger woman and made the old one look more bizarre.

"One more dumpling?" Suzette asked.

"Pig" said the mother as she placed it in her dish. Surely insults would make the girl go, but she stayed. "Why are you *ici?*" she finally asked.

"I need to see my future." Suzette was finished talking in French.

"You know how hard that is. I am old now. Too old. Go away." the last words were spoken with her hands across her face as if she wanted the girl gone before she dropped them away from her eyes. There was no movement in the room until the old woman got up and walked out the back door. Suzette went to the taxi and gave the driver some more money and a promise of more so he would not leave her here.

Paschette came back to the room smoking a strange pipe and Suzette recalled the smell as the last one she had of her mother twenty-one years ago. It took almost an hour for Paschette to prepare the drugs and ingest enough for the trance the girl was demanding.

'*Ici.*" she pointed to the patio off the kitchen where two chairs were pulled so the mother and child would be touching knees as they sat. Suzette drew a tumbler of rum, drank it, and leaned her head back to wait for her mother's vision. The rum made her head swim, but it also made it possible to wait by dissolving time. She was almost asleep when her mother's soft, pleasant voice brought her back to the patio and the feeling of hard knees pressing hers.

"Suzette" she said and the soft comfort in the sound embraced her, as if her mother cared—as if *she* cared if her mother cared.

"You saw him dead before he came here, didn't you?"

"*Oui, mon mere.*"

"The snake eyes got you, as I said long ago"

"*Non.* You are wrong."

"Snake eyes—dice. You did not avoid the dice and got hurt. I warned you."

"No. I've no problem with dice." Suzette had never been a gambler, she did not roll dice and could not remember getting in trouble over dice.

The seer struggled to go deeper and the sounds coming from her were as if she were wrestling a giant. "Dice is a woman."

Suzette saw the message very clearly. She had to admit, her mother was right. "*Oui*, a woman named Dicey but called Dice by David." Suzette admitted to herself, Dicey was the trouble that ended everything for her and David. And her mother had warned her when she was a child.

"What do you see beyond today?"

"Yghhh. *Pas plus*. There is nothing more." Suzette had some powers of her own and she knew that her mother saw more. Paschette had to tell her what she saw. Suzette had to know.

"*Ecoute moi*. "Ecoute moi. I must know. I will not leave until this is done." Pachette did not want to tell her daughter what she saw. It was too painful even for the tough old woman. She screamed and screamed, but Suzette only waited. The vision had to be told or it would haunt her mother forever. Untold visions can even kill. Paschette was scared for herself and for her daughter. Fear washed down to Paschette's knees and passed to Suzette. The girl trembled. Everything got quiet, even the breeze stopped, so the smoke from the pipe covered the two women like a fog and Suzette became dizzy with the smoke and the rum.

Slowly Paschette took the pipe from her mouth and raised her bloody eyes. "You are me and I am you. You will never find the right man to save you from yourself. Just as I sold—you will sell the only worthwhile thing you have, yourself . . . and like a slave, you will sell over and over. Your beauty will be as the smoke from my pipe. Your skin will darken in time like the horizon. Food will be plentiful and you will not be in the rain . . . but, you will be alone. You will thirst, and your skin will dry." Her voice trailed off, became difficult to hear. Suzette leaned forward as Paschette took her chin in hand and held her gaze. "Look at me Suzette and see yourself." It was a terrible sentence, and the drawing of it rendered Paschette unconscious.

Suzette stumbled to the taxi and paid the driver to take her back to the Grand Hotel where she would find the man in the bar and begin to be as her mother said. *David could save me*, she thought but he was upstairs preparing to die.

* * *

The cell phone awakened David at 8:15. "Dad, you told me to call when I landed. Which hotel?"

"Patrick, I'm glad you're here. Come to the Grand Hotel, room 806." David got up and drank the deadly elixir. The deed was done. His son would not be able to change the outcome. Then he showered and dressed to wait for his son.

David and Patrick had had an amazing relationship through the years. Although they were far removed from each other, they had established a rapport that included mutual trust and respect. David had always been honest with the boy, keeping none of his activities a secret. He was truthful about the reasons their family fell apart and exposed his own blame to his son, teaching him about mistakes, accountability, and consequences. Patrick understood he could not be with his father physically but did all he could, following his father's example, to keep the lines between them honest and strong. David flew to California for every important event in the boy's life, the last being the birth of his first daughter last year. When Patrick was told of his father's brain tumor, he flew to Maryland over his father's urging for him to stay at home with his family. It was difficult to leave before he came out of the coma and surely, if he had known at the time about the cancer, he would have risked his job to stay longer. The boy would have a father for twelve more hours and six of them would be passed watching him sleep his life away.

* * *

David tried to plan special things for the last days with Dicey, but he was feeling too badly, and the coughing had become exhausting. She tried to talk him out of making the trip, but he would not discuss it with her, and she knew she could not change his mind. His determination to go was

*the only energizing thing she saw him do . . . and so she resigned herself to
helping him get ready.*

*David wanted to take her to old familiar places, but they had to settle
for quiet time at home. The things they did were quite ordinary for her,
but he had never done them. For instance, he did the prep for their meals.
He had never cleaned carrots or peeled onions. He washed lettuce and
learned to dry it. He learned to pound a cutlet and bread a chicken breast
with such zeal that the meal tasted better to him. He rested three times a
day, so he would have the energy to be in the kitchen for each meal. Dicey
and David folded laundry together and he even iced the oatmeal cookies.
He loved every minute and she loved watching him find new pleasures
in the simple domestic chores of life. Teasing and making light of the
important things they were doing each day was sport. She often rejected
his work, and he often complained that she was a slave driver. Each dared
the other to get someone else. In this way they laughed, worked, and passed
the last days in domestic bliss.*

*On Monday evening, he got serious and although she did not want to
be serious, she did not stop him. If he thought this was the right moment,
she had to go with it.*

*"Dice, I have been thinking of what is going to happen to me. You
know I have been getting all my affairs in order."*

"Yes, I know. Do you need any help?"

*"No, it is all done, and I have talked to Patrick many times. I didn't
want to bother you about them. It is all together in that envelope on my
desk"*

*He paused, as if he were marshaling his thoughts. "Dicey, I have a
request."*

"Anything."

*"Could we have our good-bye tonight, before I leave tomorrow, while
I am feeling good? We have had a wonderful time in the kitchen, the meal
was fantastic and I am so happy. Later, a good-bye could be strained and
not so pleasant. I am not coughing tonight and I can hold you close and
enjoy just being here with you."*

*She answered with her body by sitting with him on the sofa. Her
hand gently rubbed his knee as he bent to kiss her. The pain in his chest
was abated by her caress as she put her hand in his flannel shirt. The
worry in his mind was calmed by her gentle words of love and devotion.
"I never thought we could live together and be this happy."*

"I couldn't see what you saw in me. I have always wondered why you kept me so close through the years."

"I am the only person you allowed to know you."

The fear in his soul was quieted by her assurance of his worth. He told her of the truth he had learned by reading the Bible, and asked her to read his two favorite chapters from Isaiah that gave the promise of redemption, and the Gospel of John that spoke of love and the mansion of many rooms. "Can you believe that even I can have the grace of God by just asking for it?"

"Yes, I can believe that, and I am happy that you can, too."

They sat quietly and she thought he was sleeping, but he was only resting for a minute. "I have told God that I am sorry for the wrong things I have done and for the things I should have done, but didn't. I also thanked him for you."

Those words were the most comforting ones she had heard in all of this.

"I must go, Dice." She was not sure if he meant Haiti or death. His words did not require an answer; she just pressed his body where her hands were at the moment to let him know, whatever he meant, it was understood by her.

"Please forgive me." Again, she pressed against him to let him know that all was well between them.

"The thing I want you to remember is that I love you beyond measure and I want you to be happy."

She recalled those were the exact words Greg had said to her as he left.

CHAPTER 16

The rain beating on the windows was driven by a nor'easter. The warm summer temperature, which fed the storm, belied the cold feeling permeating her soul. When she got the call she heaved a green burning vomit. The food and then the bile wrenched her body.

David was dead. It was finished.

Her head pounded and her throat burned. It was welcomed pain. She wished for relief, and begged for it to continue. Her stomach was empty but, she continued to gag and struggled to breathe. When her strength was gone, Dicey held on to the commode to support her weakened body's reaction to love's amputation by suicide.

Did he do this terrible thing for me? The awful thought brought another bout of heaving stomach and failing knees. "David! David!" She did not realize she was screaming. Her wish to deny reality left her prostrate on the floor crying endless exhausting sobs.

When she started crying it was for everything that hurt her during her whole life. Dicey crawled to bed and cried until sleep came. A fitful dream filled most of the night. Three men were there, waiting for the others to leave so the one left could come to her. Her part in the torment was wanting all three of them. The dream turned into a nightmare when she saw Greg dissolve, and David faded away. She could not see the face of the remaining man. Hot sand made her feet burn. Casino lights made her sweat and she threw back the covers. A voice called, "Dorrie."

"It's me," she kept saying but no one took notice of her. "Where is Jacques" her dream asked.

"Jacques was never here." She felt naked and guilty, just before she came back to the wet pillow. It was still dark; the wind and rain were beating the house. Dicey rose from her bed and went to the porch. Her mind was flitting from thought to thought, nothing was tied together. She was not asleep but not awake, either. She wanted to listen to the rain and remember how Greg loved the porch when it was raining. David did not like rain; it delayed too many games and changed the probability for the odds-on winner. She did not know how Jacques felt about rain, and the lack of this knowledge brought her fresh pain.

These thoughts brought her more tears. She walked out of the shelter of the porch into the warm deluge, which could cool her sweat drenched, hot body. Her tears disappeared in the rain. Her gloom was matched and it seemed the wind in her face would never let her go forward—a direction that seemed impossible. Although the temperature stayed near 70 all night, the rain chilled her as she sat on the cement of the patio ignoring her common sense and any voice of reason. Dicey had escaped reality, at last.

*　　*　　*

Jacques found her there just before dawn. He carried her to bed where he took off her wet things, and gently towel dried her hair and caressed the curl he remembered behind her ear. Dorrie gave a quiet sigh as he lay beside her shivering body, giving her back the cocoon that she had once shed for him. The sun was breaking the horizon when she warmed and stopped shaking. Her sleep became deep and restful. He checked her forehead, which was cooler, lifted the quilt over her arms, and left her bed.

Dorrie awoke to the reality that was her grief. The sun had come back as did the terrible feeling of loss. Why did David's death bring her back to grieve for Greg? She was sure she needed a psychiatrist or at least some medication to keep her from the abyss into which she was falling. Jacques was here . . . yet she knew he hadn't been. He'd carried her and warmed her . . . yet she knew he hadn't. Her dream was of him . . . funny how a dream can inspire emotions that seem so real . . . yet are as substantial as smoke. The only thing she could raise her head and do was call Jen.

"Honey, can you come? I hate to ask but I am sick with fever and I am afraid to be alone."

Jen made arrangements, and arrived in three hours. Her mother was still in bed, asleep. She was startled to open the door and see a stranger in the great room. He raised his hands, palm upwards as a sign of submission to put her at ease, calling her name. "Jen,"

"Where is my mother?" she asked trying to keep alarm out of her voice.

"She is sleeping. I was waiting until you got here before I left. I am Jacques Marquette. Did your mother tell you about me?"

"Not much—just that you helped with David's legal things. Why are you here?'

"Did you know David is dead?"

"Yes, she called me yesterday but she sounded OK, then."

"Well she's not. I tried all day and night to get her and finally drove here. When she didn't answer the door, I went around back looking for entry and found her passed out on the patio in the rain. That is how I got in the house. She has been asleep since I got her warm." He did not tell that he used his body to warm hers.

"Thank you for all you have done"

"I will stay if you think you will need something."

Jen rushed toward the bedroom. "I am calling her doctor. I think we are fine. Please see yourself out . . . and thanks."

"May I call to check on her later?"

Jacques reluctantly left Dorrie's house, but he knew she was in good hands. It seemed too many separating miles as he drove down route 301 toward the bay bridge. Each mile away from Dorrie became more difficult and on sudden impulse, he turned south toward Dover and the beaches. He would go to Bethany and wait. *Wait for what?* he wondered. Jacques could not dismiss the image of the woman he loved, curled in a fetal position in the rain. What if he had not come? Reluctantly he credited his promise to David for his repeated effort to contact Dorrie. As he drove down the beach highway, Jacques went over the last conversation he had with David. He concluded that David knew he would be dead by the 20th. Now he understood the promise insisted upon.

The chills and fever lasted three days. Dorrie drifted in and out of sleep and took some liquids at her daughter's bidding. She did not remember going out to the porch and patio. Her dreams and reality were mixed. She heard voices calling her name and thought Jacques had come to her, but knew she must put that vision away. There were some things she needed to tell Jen.

"Honey, David went to Haiti to commit suicide. He never intended to come home again."

"Oh, Mom. Are you alright?

"No, not yet. Looking back I see all the things he did in our last days. They were wonderful but—" She broke into tears again as Jen came and held her. "—but, I can't make good memories out of those days. Will it happen? I don't know. He didn't want me to watch him die . . . and he chose this awful alternative."

"It was his choice, Mom. You hold no blame."

"I know . . . I know. If I had known what he planned, I could not have changed it."

Dorrie—she could no longer think of herself as *Dicey*—recovered her composure and found a way to go through each day. Of course she would, being a woman of great strength, but strength did not lessen the pain, it only made handling it possible. Her daughter brought her back with care and love. They talked about all the grief spilling over Dorrie's life. This new grief brought back the common loss of father and husband. "I understand why David went to Haiti, Jen. He did it to spare me the pain of his prolonged death, but more than that he would not allow his life to waste away day by day, hour by hour. And I know he doesn't want me to agonize over it. He was wrong and I will always wish he had not . . ." She could not say the words. ". . . but I understand. David could not live without his strength and it was the one thing I could not give him. It will take a while, but knowing the man, this path is obvious. He did not want me to relive losing your father and I wondered how I would do with that, too." As her head cleared, she reconciled her loss and his choice as best she could. She needed to grieve for David and let him go, and she spent her quiet moments looking for the tools to do that. It was ironic that she loved him longer than Greg but she would not grieve as long. David made it easier to go on without Greg but there was no one to ease the path without David.

"Mom, Patrick King called about you. He has been very concerned and is waiting for you to feel better so he can come to see you."

"Patrick was in Haiti with David. How hard was that? Here I am feeling sorry for myself and he lost his father. I thought he would be back to in California by now."

"No, He has brought his wife and daughter here; they are staying at the apartment."

Dorrie was delighted at this opportunity to meet David's son and his family. The expected visit brought a lift in her spirit.

"Call him. Tell him to come." *I hope I am ready for this*, she mused.

Jen helped her mother repair a week's neglect to her hair, freshen her appearance and pick a bright outfit to meet David's family. With all her outward preparation, she was not prepared for what tore her insides when the younger version of David walked to the porch where she waited. Tears sprung to her eyes and all the make-up work was to no avail.

"You look so much like your father . . . maybe a bit more handsome." she added to lighten the effect her tears had on the beautiful young family. She began to heal as they shared their grief and offered compassion. Patrick accepted her right to cry for his father.

"Hello, Dicey." He went to her immediately and embraced her. "I have wanted to meet you for so long. This is my wife, Karen and this is Olivia. She will be one-year-old in two weeks."

The visit was much easier than either party thought it would be. The delightful baby added a beautiful touch to a family that seemed to be pulling together and including her. She asked about his mother, Patti, and recalled some old school memories to help with the connection. They talked of the future and Jen invited them to her home someday when little Olivia would be old enough to appreciate the beautiful Delaware beaches. Food was brought to the porch and eating together did the usual amazing job of making friends of strangers. When Jen took Karen in to find a napping place for the child, Patrick had the time he was seeking to be alone with Dicey. He could tell her some of the things she needed to know.

"I hope it is alright to call you Dicey? That is who you are to me," Her happy smile and nod of consent urge him to go on. "Good! Dicey, if and when you are ready to hear the story of Dad's last day, I will tell you. I don't think we are ready for that now."

"Thank you, Patrick."

"There are a few things Dad asked me to do. You know how direct and adamant he was about his choices. Are you ready to hear these things? I don't want to rush you." Again she nodded, not trusting her voice. "Let me just say, he made it very clear to me that his love for you was the most important thing in his life. Everything he did in the last months, every decision was with you in mind."

Dicey sat quietly and it was the warm appealing way of the young man facing her that made it possible for her to stay in her chair, waiting and listening. "First, he changed his will. You are not executor, I am. He did not want to leave that burden on you. He made it very clear to me that you are only to remember the times you were together and not any of this legal stuff that has to be taken care of now. He repeatedly used the phrase, 'Set her free.'"

Dicey remembered the times he used that phrase in their last days. Of course he would be true to his word and do just that.

"Dicey, you do not have to come to the reading of the will. You do not have to see Suzette, and you do not have to clean out his personal things from the apartment. He told me to ask if there are things you want from the apartment and see that you get them." He looked at her with a questioning look.

"I would like the photo album; that is all . . . . oh, Patrick, there is something else . . . he had an old photograph of his mother that he carried in his wallet. I would love to have a copy of that to put in the frame with his picture there on my mantle." she replied while still digesting what he was saying. The weight off her shoulders was tremendous and the love she had for David was reiterated in his final actions. *Thank you, my darling*, was all she could think as the necessity to return to Maryland was removed.

"I have read the will. He said you refused to be named in it and you are not."

"I know."

"Officially, you have no connection to David King, but because of the things he told me in Haiti, I know your connection to my father was great and something I will always be indebted for."

"Patrick, don't thank me for loving your father; love is thanks enough. We shared life in a very unusual way. Most people would never understand, but it seems your father was able to explain it to you so you could offer me great comfort today. I thank you." The afternoon was flying away and she knew her visitors would soon have to go. While they were with her, she sat close to Patrick and enjoyed the reminder he was of his father. It was easy to let them go for she was sure that in the coming years she would hear from this man who wanted to know more about his father . . . and she was the only one who could tell him. Amid their good-byes, Pat was holding back and gave Karen a sign to take Olivia and go on to the car without him.

"I have saved something for the last moments of this visit. Dad gave me this to give to you. Please take it." He reached into his pocket and came out with a small box. "You know he could only express his feelings in material things, so in that spirit, take this." He opened the box to reveal a large uncut, unset diamond. "'Tell her, this is me until she shaped me and put me in the right setting'—those were his words."

Dicey could only look at the stone and then at the man handing it to her. When the stone tumbled into her palm, her mind drifted, and for a moment, David himself stood beside her. Dicey had a sweet pang of joy.

Patrick watched her carefully, and allowed her to return to him. "He feared you would not take it. If he can see us, he is pleased." He closed her fingers around the stone just as David would have done, if he were here.

"Here is his letter to you." He placed an envelope on the foyer table and took her in his arms. "Take care of yourself. I will call you before I go home."

She stood in the doorway with the diamond in her closed hand and the feeling of David's arms around her; the spell would be broken if she moved or took a breath.

*　　*　　*

David wrote the letter the day he got his diagnosis from Dr. Drysdale. Of the many things he had to do, this was the most important and most difficult. He was not good at writing or expressing himself . . . . but he took pen in hand and wrote as it came to him.

> *Dicey,*
> *I do not know why you have stayed with me all my life but if you hadn't I would have been lost long ago. You have been a part of every decision I ever made—the good and the bad. I*

135

always thought about how you would feel about what I was doing. I know when you approved and when you disapproved. It didn't change many choices but it did keep me from making some very bad ones, which are better not mentioned. But, mostly, I knew you would love me no matter what. Sometimes I thought that is how a mother loves but how would I know about that? Make no mistake, I never thought of you as my mother. You have been my anchor. You are my winnings, my best bet, my pat hand and my sure thing.

I have gotten smarter over the years, and it took me a long time to realize that my marriages failed because I wanted you all along. I loved you and wanted you but by then you were happy with Greg. I have loved you so much that I was content knowing you were happy with him. Believe me, it was my biggest loss. Dice, I loved you enough not to let you be bound to my life. Now if this diagnosis of cancer is as bad as it seems, I know you will be reading this at my death. I want this to be a love note. We don't have to worry about the things we never said. I think we always said the most important things to each other. The hardest thing is leaving you.

Please be happy. Your smile lights the world; it always did mine.

Love,
David

Folded in the envelope was a scrap of paper, not as neat and although it was David's writing, it was not as flowing as the first letter. She knew he wrote it four days ago.

Dice,

Remember the good-bye we had at the apartment. I do. My last thought will be us on the sofa with your hand inside my shirt feeling my heart and soothing my lungs. Forgive me for leaving this way. If you can forgive me, you will go on with your life and be happy. I know you will always grieve for Greg; do not do that for me. Remember my crazy life was good because of you. Tell my story. You are the only one who really knew it. I love you with my last breath.

Be happy, my love.

D

At the bottom in weak and hardly legible scratching, he wrote again:

"*Be happy*" *and drew a crooked heart.*

CHAPTER 17

J en watched her mother come back into the world with interest in her home and family, but she could see Dorrie had lost a spark.

"Mom, I just asked if you wanted orange juice."

"Sorry, Jen. I wasn't listening. A small glass, please."

Try as she would to persuade her to come home with her, she refused. Although her willingness to talk about David put Jen at ease about her mother's grief, there was something she could not put her finger on. At times, it was as if her mother was in another world and had to be called back to her meal, the TV show, and even the conversations they were having. It was time to address what was going on here. "Mother," she started, which got Dorrie's attention as she seldom addressed her so formally, "I wish I knew what is on your mind that is distracting you so much. Are you going to need some help dealing with David's suicide?"

"Dear," she paused for the right words. "I am reconciled to that. His life was over and if he had come back from Haiti the time would have been terrible. I cannot think that he committed suicide for me—it would be too much to bear. I believe he would have done that one way or another." She gave a deep sigh—resigned to the hopelessness David faced. "There was no way David could have wasted away. If I don't put his decision out of my mind, it will be as if I couldn't forgive him. No, I have already gone to our good memories. I miss him terribly and often catch myself thinking he will call or I will call him, but that is normal. It isn't as if I miss him here around this house as I miss your father every day."

"You won't come home with me and I am not sure you are ready to be alone, yet."

"I will be fine. Go home and I will plan a visit sometime soon. I need to stay here, by myself. I really do. And you, my dear, are needed by your family."

"Tell me what you are thinking about when you drift away from here." Jen wanted answers before she could, with good conscience, leave her mother. Dorrie understood that she would have to talk about the things that were disrupting her ability to pick up her quiet country club life.

"To be honest, I go back to the dream I had the night I got sick. Some parts are so real they won't leave me. I am having trouble sorting what happened and what I dreamed. Maybe I need to forget everything about that night." She paused to decide if she wanted to tell Jen about Jacques. Maybe it would help to cross that boundary and expose the pain. "I never told you everything about Jacques Marquette. You never met him—"

"Yes, I did." Jen interrupted.

"You did?"

"He was here when I arrived Friday morning."

"What are you saying?" She was having trouble with this news. *Surely Jen was mistaken.* Her confused stare led Jen to explain.

"Mom, when I opened the door, he was sitting right there—" she pointed, "—in that chair. He was the one who carried you in from the rain and put you to bed. He tried to call you that whole day and night. He said he came here because he couldn't get an answer. Maybe you should call and thank him for what he did. I am sorry I didn't mention it sooner . . . so much going on with you, and Patrick's visit." Jen noticed the astonished look on her mother's face. "He called one more time to ask about you, and said David's son had taken care of the business he thought he had with you. Legal stuff—I . . . I didn't want to bother you."

Dorrie's head spun with the things Jen was saying—things that fit into her confusion, illusions, and dreams. *Jacques was here.*

"Did he say anything else?"

"No, only that he hoped you were doing well . . . and something about living at the beach."

Jen leaned forward, toward her mother. "Is all this important, Mom? Aren't you relieved of all legal obligations for David? Am I missing something? Do you need to talk to this lawyer?"

"Oh, Jen." Dorrie took her hand and drew her closer. "Come here and sit while I tell you a long story." She told her daughter about her time with Jacques and the choice she made for David. She felt very old, even a bit ridiculous, as she tried to tell her daughter of her feelings. How does a woman with grandchildren explain passion and love to her daughter? It is well known that grown children ignore their parents' sex life. Could her daughter understand that not only was passion important until her father's death, it had been renewed with another man almost two decades later?

"How can I tell it so you understand . . ." A deep breath helped her to go on. "Jen, I behaved badly and hurt him without explaining. I said a final good bye and chose David. It is as simple as that. But I will always remember our time together. Jacques helped me to define my devotion to David. He showed me that life was much more than moving in and out of David's world."

"I would love to thank the man who finally made you see what I have been telling you for years." She reached over to give a bear hug and to smile generously at her mother.

Dorrie was mistaken in thinking Jen would take this lightly. Jen did not see it that way at all. She did not miss the light that sparkled in her mother's eye or the smile that had not surfaced for days until she began talking of Jacques Marquette. She also saw the deep sadness when her mother concluded. "I am so sorry for what I did to Jacques but I had no choice."

Jen brought it all down to one question. "Do you want to see him again?"

There was only one answer to that . . . but did she have the courage? Until she was told that Jacques came to her, she never considered seeing him again. And yet, she was not going to re-evaluate every thought, every option. Nothing really changed. One phone call, relating to David's business, did not mean he could forgive her.

Yet, he had come to her, cared for her . . . .

"I hurt him badly when I went back to David. I know he was sure I would not go, but I did. It was unforgiveable. I can't forgive myself, how can I expect him to?"

She did not answer Jen's question about seeing Jacques. She could not.

Jen rocked her mother like a baby, with arms that were usually on the receiving end.

"Think it over, Mom. You always told me things are never so black and white that we can't paint a Technicolor version. Right?"

"I said that, yet now . . . I don't believe my own words." She looked at her daughter. "Jen, go home. I have thought this over for weeks. It is time for me to settle down where I belong. I have been very happy here and I will be again. My friends are calling me to rejoin activities. That is what I am going to do. I can't run to David for diversion any more. I'm sure Jacques has moved on, and that is what I must do, too."

*   *   *

In Delaware everything was easy, even doing nothing was easy. Life was full of acceptance. Acceptance of the status quo. Acceptance that age was the only leveler. Acceptance that many things take too much time and effort. Acceptance that maybe there is no time left. If all the important things happened in the past, that was where conversations center. It was quite possible that if Dorrie had met Jacques here, without the mystic of David, he might not have given her a second glance and she most certainly would not have had a romantic notion about him. Life in her Delaware retirement community was not about doing the unexpected.

David's death changed Dorrie. The last few weeks scrambled her. She felt cracked, beaten, and changed. The happiness she felt with Jacques on the beach seemed a fantasy and she discarded it as easily as David discarded his own life—without thinking of the consequences for the one left behind. Life is not all fun, it is not pretend and diversion. It is death and loss of opportunities, and at her age it is very tiring.

Jacques saw Dorrie and she saw him—not colored by years nor tempered by location. He wanted all the time they had stretched out before them, but she'd refused to give it to him. Her time with Jacques made a treasured memory and she would settle for that. Her chance was gone and she would let it go. Dorrie got up from these revelries and checked the calendar for the Dominos game at the clubhouse. Sometimes the easiest thing to do is nothing.

A week went by and life did settle down. Jen called to get her mother's report on the ladies luncheon yesterday and the book club today. She put enthusiasm in her voice to satisfy her daughter, but she was lying. The so-called normal life was not keeping her mind from Jacques. It wandered from conversations to his smile, and from loneliness to his touch. *I have to keep trying,* she told herself. The nights were the worst. Every night she woke in the wee hours and found her rest was over. With her memories of the beach, she could go to the wonder of her time with Jacques, but she had to face that things were not getting better. She had not moved on.

Dorrie called Jen to discussed selling and starting fresh in a condominium in Frederick. "Mom, it is too soon to make a decision. Are you really ready to make such a big change?" Dorrie thought about Jen's question and knew *change* was the problem. That night she left her bed and gave herself a lecture, chastising herself in the mirror. "What would you change your life for Dorrie? You didn't change it for David. You had your life and David too. Did you think you could come and go like that with Jacques? He isn't waiting for you, Stupid. There is no ticket in and out of his life. No red dresses, no wigs—just real life with real choices. Jacques is not David." Her own reflection demanded honesty. "Jacques wanted you, just as you are." The tears started. "I know . . . I know . . ." she sobbed looking straight into the red, sad eyes of her soul. ". . . but I would change everything for him," she whispered. Exhausted, she returned to her bed.

The long dark night went on; the clock moved to 3:56 and she watched each minute as it passed to 4:00.

Dorrie got up and dressed in sweatshirt and pants. She drew her hair up in a comb and gathered some sandals and a blanket to go out in the hot August night. She drove south without a plan. Her headlights lit the sign—*Beaches 45 Miles.* By the time she approached Bethany, there was a glow in the eastern sky. All the homes in Blue Heron Dunes were dark. She parked in a no parking zone, saw the warning sign—*Private Property No Beach Access,* and paused to ask herself, "What am I doing?" before stepping on the sand.

The blanket was spread on the beach, her sandals were kicked off, and her toes dug in to find the warm sand just below the surface. There was a great comfort beside the ocean where the surf comes and comes again to wash the shore. The gritty sand and gentle surf scoured David's pain away. The promise she made to herself the morning she left Jacques was broken. She watched for the sunrise, awaiting its certainty and its promise . . . rejoicing that she had arrived in time . . .

fearing that if she had been too late something important would stay dark.

The sky lightened and Dorrie experienced a peace she had not felt since she got the call from Haiti.

She talked to Greg. "I lied, sweetheart. I can't do this alone. It is too terrible. Now I know why I ran to David—being lonely is a sentence that is too long and bitter." She thought a moment about the words she had uttered and continued with the next thought. "Remembering our good life makes me want more." Pink paths from the horizon streaked across the dark sky.

She talked to David. "Good bye, David. You will always be a part of me, but we never really belonged to each other. We had to say *I love you*—all the time. True lovers do not have to do that." She put his name in the salt air one last time, "David." Coral hues lit the ocean clouds from behind.

She began to cry as she tried to speak to Jacques. "I . . . I . . . I am so sorry." Her words twisted and turned in the morning breeze like a butterfly's flight. As the early light trailed a golden path across the water, she dried her tears with a sandy hand that scratched her cheeks. Dorrie lifted a single grain from her face, held it between her fingers and marveled. She was a grain of sand on this shore, by this enormous ocean, and her excuses for not seizing life became insignificant. A new perspective came as the sun's slight crescent broke the plane of the horizon. All at once she knew with absolute certainty that she was failing Greg and David. They loved life and they wanted her to love it—all the more because they had left it to her and believed she would. They expected her to run *into the wind* for lift when she needed it, to run *with the wind* to make her flight easier, and to *ignore crosswinds* of fear and cowardice.

"Bend, don't break." She chastised herself as she watched the dune grass bend to the breeze that always stirred when the sun breached the horizon.

In the house above the dune, Jacques turned toward the window to see the rising sun. He leaned up on one elbow and saw the figure silhouetted on the beach. At that moment, the woman stood, turned her back to the east and looked at the third row of windows in his bedroom. She waved and beckoned to him. Jacques did not take time to put on shoes. He leaped over the balcony railing and ran to her blanket.

Dorrie waited until he was close enough to see his smile before she ran to his open arms. "Jacques, I do love you."

"I know," he said before he kissed her.

Later that night she thanked him for coming to rescue her in her darkest hour. "Dorrie, I came because David made me promise to call you and bring the escrow settlement. On *that* day—he insisted. It was the last thing he said to me when he came to my office. You remember; you waited in the car and he kissed you while I was at the window. I was jealous." He smiled and kissed her again.

"David took my marker on it. 'Call Dicey on the 20th—don't give up until you talk to her.' I had no idea what that meant, but now we both know, he sent me to you. He gave me his winnings, his best bet, his pat hand and his sure thing—you."

*   *   *

She wished they would always be sitting in row four, seats five and six. She wanted him to chase her over the playground. She wanted him to ask her out on a date and kiss her like he meant it.

Instead, she grew up.

They could not go back to those school days. He loved her enough not to gamble on her chance to be happy. It had to be a sure thing.

The End

Book Club and Reading Group Discussion Topics

1. What are the factors that made it possible for Dicey to step out from the comfortable retirement community into David's world?

2. What kind of man was David King? Was Dicey honest in her evaluation or did she have blinders where he was concerned? What did you find appealing about him? Discuss gambling in our society. Do you agree it is a matter of geography? Was David a criminal?

3. Why was David dangerous? Could you move in his world? What would be your dilemmas if you were Dicey?

4. When Dicey described her grief for her husband (page 94), did it give you new incite? On page 106, the author describes death. What are your comments on this?

5. Were you surprised at how quickly Jacques Marquette captured Dicey's attention? Do you question how fast their affair advanced? Evaluate age in their love equation.

6. Each of the main characters (except Jacques) seemed to have conflicting lives. Discuss the two lives of each—David, Suzette and Dicey. Is the author stretching the truth or do most people portray themselves in multiple ways throughout their lives. Of the three, who had the most conflicted life and who was closest to presenting his/her life as a whole?

7. Why did David King chose suicide?

8. Find the similarities between Suzette and her mother, Paschette. Did you feel any compassion for either one of them, or both?

9. Discuss Jacques opinion that Dicey used David King as a safety blanket.

10. The theme of this book is the timelessness of romantic connection. Do you believe time runs out? What factors prohibit finding new love and new life after age 60? What factors make it possible?

11. Who took the biggest gamble in this book?

12. Discuss the author's use of the uncut diamond and the sunrise to portray her main characters.